iHuman
新民説

成为更好的人

鲍勃 · 迪伦诗歌集

像一块滚石

[美] 鲍勃 · 迪伦　著

包慧怡　马世芳　李皖　胡续冬　奚密　译

GUANGXI NORMAL UNIVERSITY PRESS
广西师范大学出版社
· 桂林 ·

XIANG YI KUAI GUNSHI

LYRICS: 1961-2012

著作权合同登记号桂图登字：20-2017-053 号

图书在版编目（CIP）数据

鲍勃·迪伦诗歌集：1961—2012. 像一块滚石：汉英对照／（美）鲍勃·迪伦著；包慧怡等译. —桂林：广西师范大学出版社，2017.6

书名原文：LYRICS：1961-2012

ISBN 978-7-5495-9685-0

Ⅰ. ①鲍… Ⅱ. ①鲍…②包… Ⅲ. ①诗集—美国—现代—汉、英 Ⅳ. ①I712.25

中国版本图书馆 CIP 数据核字（2017）第 078982 号

出　版：广西师范大学出版社
　　　　广西桂林市中华路 22 号　邮政编码：541001
网　址：http://www.bbtpress.com
出版人：张艺兵
发　行：广西师范大学出版社
　　　　电话：（0773）2802178
印　刷：山东临沂新华印刷物流集团有限责任公司印刷
　　　　山东临沂高新技术产业开发区新华路
　　　　邮政编码：276017
开　本：740 mm × 1 092 mm　1/32
印　张：8　　字数：90 千字
版　次：2017 年 6 月第 1 版　　2017 年 6 月第 1 次
定　价：25.00 元

目 录

重访 61 号公路

金发叠金发

约翰·韦斯利·哈丁

1. Of war an peace/ the truth does twist/ it's curfew gull just glides/
upon the fungus forest cloud, the cowboy Angel rides
An tho he lights his candle in the sun ~~his candle burns the day~~, it's glow is waxed in black
All ecpt when neath the trees of eden —

2. The lamppost stands with folded arms/ it's ~~[illegible]~~ iron claws attached
+ the curbs neath wailing babys — tho it's shadow's metal badge/
All in all, can only fall, with a crashing but meaningless blow
No sound comes from the depths of eden —

3. the savage soldier sticks his head in sand an then complains
unto the shoeless hunter/who's grown deaf but still remains
upon the beach where hound dogs bay at ships with tattoed sails
heading for the gates of eden —

4. With his time rusted compass blade, Alladin an his Lamp
sits with utopian hermit monks side saddle on the golden calf
An on their promises of paradise, you will not hear a laugh
exept inside the gates of eden —

5. the motorcycle black madonna/ two wheeled gypsy queen
an her silver studded phantom cause the grey flannel dwarf + scream
As he weeps + wicked birds of prey, who pick up his bread crumb sins
there are no sins once in the gates of eden —
(smile)

6. relationships of ~~[illegible]~~ ownership wait outside the wings
of those ~~[illegible]~~ condemned + act accordingly ~~[illegible]~~ + waiting for ~~[illegible]~~ succeeding kings
An I try + harmonize ~~[illegible]~~ with songs/ the lonesome sparrow sings
~~[illegible]~~ All men are kings inside the gates of eden —

7. the kingdoms of experience/in the precious wind they rot
while paupers change possessions/each wishing for what the other's got
An the princess an the prince discuss what is real an what is not
it doesnt matter inside the gates of eden —

8. the foreign sun/it rises/ on a house that is not mine
As friends an other strangers from their fates try to resign
Leaving men wholly total free + do anything they wish but die
There's no where + hide inside the gates of eden

9. At dawn my lover comes t me an tells me of her dreams

At times i think/there are no words, but these + tell
no truths,

重访 61 号公路
Highway 61 Revisited

包慧怡　译

这是鲍勃·迪伦的第六张专辑，发行于 1965 年 8 月 30 日。标题中的“61 号公路”即美国 61 号国家公路，北起明尼苏达州怀俄明市，沿密西西比河，南下至路易斯安那州新奥尔良市，穿过众多蓝调音乐家之乡，因而不少蓝调作品以此路为主题。迪伦在自传《编年史：第一卷》（*Chronicles.Volume One*）中提到，他总觉得自己是从这条公路起步，一直在这条路上，且可以自此通向任何地方。

如果说《全数带回家》是迪伦进行“插电”的初步尝试，那么这张专辑则是开启他摇滚时代的标志。彼时英国披头士、滚石风头正盛，而作为摇滚发源地的美国自“猫王”后相形失色。巡演归来的迪伦打破了这一局面，将新的摇滚气息注入传统蓝调与民谣，“以摇滚的态度玩儿民谣”，开创了民谣摇滚的音乐形式。

这张专辑，将兰波和凯鲁亚克的影响叠加再造，融合西部片、公路片特有的狂放和戏谑，塑造了超现实主义的诡谲梦境。罪人、恶棍、怪人、英雄等角色出没于“61号公路”，隐秘地上演一场荒诞、罪恶、喧哗的狂欢。不过，在一连串看似光怪陆离的魔幻景象中，迪伦并未从现实关切中抽离，反而拓宽了抗议歌曲的意涵，如《墓碑蓝调》以荒谬的形式展现持续升级的越战，《荒芜巷》以隐喻的手法指涉纳粹对犹太人的屠戮。

专辑中，最为知名的无疑是《像一块滚石》。这首歌在不被看好的情况下，意外成为最能代表迪伦的经典之一。歌中的“像一块滚石”，道出无处可归、滚动前行的迷茫，引起试图挣脱主流文化束缚、按自己意志生活的一代人的深深共鸣。

此专辑在《滚石》杂志评选出的史上最佳五百张专辑中位列第一。英国乐评人迈克尔·格雷（Michael Gray）更称，整个摇滚文化、整个“后披头士”流行摇滚世界，乃至某种意义上的20世纪60年代，都从这里开始。

编者

像一块滚石

那会儿你衣着光鲜
正当年，扔给乞丐一毛钱，对吧？
别人给你打电话："宝贝留神，你准得栽跟头"
你觉得他们在说笑
你老是嘲笑那些
游手好闲的家伙
现在你没声儿了吧
现在你不神气了吧
当你得为下顿饭东奔西跑

感觉如何
感觉如何
无家可归
像个彻头彻尾的陌生人
像一块滚石？

没错，孤傲小姐，你上过最高级的学校
可你很清楚，你不过在那儿醉生梦死
没人教会你怎么在街头求生
现在你发现非习惯这境遇不可

你说你永远不会向那些
神叨叨的流浪汉低头，如今你意识到
他可不是在贩卖托词
当你瞪着他眼中的虚空
问他想不想做一桩买卖？

感觉如何
感觉如何
孤苦伶仃
没有回家的路
像个彻头彻尾的陌生人
像一块滚石？

你从不曾转身看杂耍人和小丑皱起的眉头
当他们走来给你变把戏
你从来不明白这样不对头
你不该让别人帮你找乐子
你习惯和你的外交官一起骑铬马
他肩头还坐着一只暹罗猫
他可真是今非昔比
发现这一点是不是特难受
当他从你那儿把一切都偷走

感觉如何
感觉如何
孤苦伶仃
没有回家的路
像个彻头彻尾的陌生人
像一块滚石？

高塔上的公主啊，所有时髦人物
他们酩酊大醉，自命成功人士
把各种珍贵礼物交换来交换去
但你现在得取下钻石戒指，宝贝你得当掉它
你过去嘲笑拿破仑的
褴褛衣衫和寒碜谈吐
现在去他那儿吧，他叫你呢，你拒绝不了
你现在什么也没有，没什么可失去
你现在是个隐形人，没啥秘密要保护

感觉如何
感觉如何
孤苦伶仃
没有回家的路
像个彻头彻尾的陌生人
像一块滚石？

Like a Rolling Stone

Once upon a time you dressed so fine
You threw the bums a dime in your prime, didn't you?
People'd call, say, "Beware doll, you're bound to fall"
You thought they were all kiddin' you
You used to laugh about
Everybody that was hangin' out
Now you don't talk so loud
Now you don't seem so proud
About having to be scrounging for your next meal

How does it feel
How does it feel
To be without a home
Like a complete unknown
Like a rolling stone?

You've gone to the finest school all right, Miss Lonely
But you know you only used to get juiced in it
And nobody has ever taught you how to live on the street
And now you find out you're gonna have to get used to it
You said you'd never compromise
With the mystery tramp, but now you realize
He's not selling any alibis
As you stare into the vacuum of his eyes
And ask him do you want to make a deal?

How does it feel
How does it feel
To be on your own

With no direction home
Like a complete unknown
Like a rolling stone?

You never turned around to see the frowns on the jugglers
and the clowns
When they all come down and did tricks for you
You never understood that it ain't no good
You shouldn't let other people get your kicks for you
You used to ride on the chrome horse with your diplomat
Who carried on his shoulder a Siamese cat
Ain't it hard when you discover that
He really wasn't where it's at
After he took from you everything he could steal

How does it feel
How does it feel
To be on your own
With no direction home
Like a complete unknown
Like a rolling stone?

Princess on the steeple and all the pretty people
They're drinkin', thinkin' that they got it made
Exchanging all kinds of precious gifts and things
But you'd better lift your diamond ring, you'd better pawn
it babe
You used to be so amused
At Napoleon in rags and the language that he used
Go to him now, he calls you, you can't refuse
When you got nothing, you got nothing to lose
You're invisible now, you got no secrets to conceal

How does it feel
How does it feel
To be on your own
With no direction home
Like a complete unknown
Like a rolling stone?

墓碑蓝调

当然了，甜心们现在都躺在床上
城市政要们正试图批准
保罗·列维尔的马儿转生[1]
但小城大可不必紧张

贝尔·斯塔尔[2]的幽灵把智慧传递给
修女耶洗别[3]，她为开膛手杰克
猛力织一顶秃假发，杰克他
端坐在商会的头把交椅上

妈妈在工厂里
她没有鞋子
爸爸在巷道里
寻找保险丝

1.1775 年 4 月 18 日，美国独立战争中第一场战役的前夕，英军计划发动突袭，银匠保罗·列维尔得知后午夜策马赶赴列克星敦预警。

2. 贝尔·斯塔尔（Belle Starr，1848—1889），具有传奇色彩的美国西部女匪，从事过马贼、走私等各种违法营生，有“强盗女王”之称。

3. 耶洗别，《旧约·列王记》中以色列王亚哈的妻子，崇拜异教，迫害先知以利亚，后被喻指歹毒的女人。

我在大街上
听着墓碑蓝调

歇斯底里的新娘，在投币游乐场
尖叫着呻吟："我被坑大了！"
再把医生传唤，他拉下卷帘门：
"我建议别让小伙子们进来"

现在巫医驾到，拖脚上前
趾高气扬，把新娘嘱咐：
"停止哭泣，咽下你的骄傲
你不会死，这不是毒药"

妈妈在工厂里
她没有鞋子
爸爸在巷道里
寻找保险丝
我在大街上
听着墓碑蓝调

施洗约翰，折磨完窃贼
抬头看看英雄，总司令官
"告诉我，大英雄，但请长话短说

有没有一个洞容我吐一吐？”

总司令官边追苍蝇，边回答：
“鬼哭狼嚎的人都去死吧！”
他扔下一只杠铃，指向天：
“太阳不是黄色，是只鸡崽”[1]

妈妈在工厂里
她没有鞋子
爸爸在巷道里
寻找保险丝
我在大街上
听着墓碑蓝调

非利士人之王，赶去救大兵
把腮骨放上墓石，装饰他们的坟墓[2]
把花衣笛手关进大牢，喂肥奴隶
然后把他们一个个送进丛林

吉普赛人戴维高举吹灯，烧掉兵营

---

1. 黄色，俚语有“怯懦”之意。鸡崽，俚语有“懦夫”之意。
2.《旧约·士师记》15:11-17，参孙用驴腮骨杀了一千非利士人。

身后跟着佩德罗，他忠实的奴仆
他大摇大摆，带着丰硕的集邮成果
去赢得友谊，并影响大叔[1]

妈妈在工厂里
她没有鞋子
爸爸在巷道里
寻找保险丝
我在大街上
听着墓碑蓝调

天真的几何，皮包骨
迫使伽利略的数学课本被扔向
大利拉[2]，她一文不值，独自枯坐
脸颊上的泪珠来自欢笑

但愿我能给比尔兄弟来桩大刺激
我会用链子把他锁在山顶，再找来

---

1. 大叔，可能是代表美国的绰号“山姆大叔”（Uncle Sam）。
2. 大利拉，《圣经》中为参孙所爱者，后经非利士人的首领利诱，出卖了参孙力量的秘密。

一堆立柱，还有塞西尔 · B. 德米尔[1]
从此他会一直死得非常快乐

妈妈在工厂里
她没有鞋子
爸爸在巷道里
寻找保险丝
我在大街上
听着墓碑蓝调

“阿妈”雷尼[2]和贝多芬曾展开铺盖的地方
大号手如今绕旗杆排练，国家银行
为了创收，贩卖灵魂指路图
养老院和大学是它的客户

现在我希望为你写一支平淡的旋律
能支撑你，亲爱的女士，远离疯狂
能抚慰你，令你镇静，为你消除

---

1. 塞西尔 · B. 德米尔（Cecil B. DeMille，1881—1959），美国电影导演，好莱坞元老级人物。《参孙与大利拉》（*Samson and Delilah*，1949）为其作品。
2. “阿妈”雷尼（Ma Rainey，1882/1886—1939），美国蓝调歌手，被誉为“蓝调之母”。

你那无用又无由的知识导致的痛苦

妈妈在工厂里

她没有鞋子

爸爸在巷道里

寻找保险丝

我在大街上

听着墓碑蓝调

Tombstone Blues

The sweet pretty things are in bed now of course
The city fathers they're trying to endorse
The reincarnation of Paul Revere's horse
But the town has no need to be nervous

The ghost of Belle Starr she hands down her wits
To Jezebel the nun she violently knits
A bald wig for Jack the Ripper who sits
At the head of the chamber of commerce

Mama's in the fact'ry
She ain't got no shoes
Daddy's in the alley
He's lookin' for the fuse
I'm in the streets
With the tombstone blues

The hysterical bride in the penny arcade
Screaming she moans, "I've just been made"
Then sends out for the doctor who pulls down the shade
Says, "My advice is to not let the boys in"

Now the medicine man comes and he shuffles inside
He walks with a swagger and he says to the bride
"Stop all this weeping, swallow your pride
You will not die, it's not poison"

Mama's in the fact'ry
She ain't got no shoes

Daddy's in the alley
He's lookin' for the fuse
I'm in the streets
With the tombstone blues

Well, John the Baptist after torturing a thief
Looks up at his hero the Commander-in-Chief
Saying, "Tell me great hero, but please make it brief
Is there a hole for me to get sick in?"

The Commander-in-Chief answers him while chasing a fly
Saying, "Death to all those who would whimper and cry"
And dropping a barbell he points to the sky
Saying, "The sun's not yellow it's chicken"

Mama's in the fact'ry
She ain't got no shoes
Daddy's in the alley
He's lookin' for the fuse
I'm in the streets
With the tombstone blues

The king of the Philistines his soldiers to save
Puts jawbones on their tombstones and flatters their graves
Puts the pied pipers in prison and fattens the slaves
Then sends them out to the jungle

Gypsy Davey with a blowtorch he burns out their camps
With his faithful slave Pedro behind him he tramps
With a fantastic collection of stamps
To win friends and influence his uncle

Mama's in the fact'ry

She ain't got no shoes
Daddy's in the alley
He's lookin' for the fuse
I'm in the streets
With the tombstone blues

The geometry of innocence flesh on the bone
Causes Galileo's math book to get thrown
At Delilah who sits worthlessly alone
But the tears on her cheeks are from laughter

Now I wish I could give Brother Bill his great thrill
I would set him in chains at the top of the hill
Then send out for some pillars and Cecil B. DeMille
He could die happily ever after

Mama's in the fact'ry
She ain't got no shoes
Daddy's in the alley
He's lookin' for the fuse
I'm in the streets
With the tombstone blues

Where Ma Rainey and Beethoven once unwrapped their bedroll
Tuba players now rehearse around the flagpole
And the National Bank at a profit sells road maps for the soul
To the old folks home and the college

Now I wish I could write you a melody so plain
That could hold you dear lady from going insane
That could ease you and cool you and cease the pain

Of your useless and pointless knowledge

Mama's in the fact'ry
She ain't got no shoes
Daddy's in the alley
He's lookin' for the fuse
I'm in the streets
With the tombstone blues

要笑不容易，要哭只须坐火车

哎，我搭乘一辆邮车，宝贝
买不到刺激
哎，我整夜没睡，宝贝
斜倚着车窗
哎，如果我死在
山坡顶上
如果我没能办到，你知道
我的宝贝会办到

妈妈[1]，月亮看起来不美吗
这穿过树梢闪耀的月亮？
妈妈，制动员看起来不美吗
当他摇旗拦下双 E 火车？
太阳看起来不美吗
当它向海面遍洒阳光？
我的姑娘看起来不美吗
当她一路追随我的脚步？

---

1. 妈妈，口语中又有“情人”“妻子”之意。

如今，凛冬将至
窗玻璃上结满了霜
我跑去告诉所有人
却没法抵达彼方
哎，我想做你的爱人，宝贝
我不想做你的上司
别说我从没警告过你
当你的火车迷失

It Takes a Lot to Laugh, It Takes a Train to Cry

Well, I ride on a mailtrain, baby
Can't buy a thrill
Well, I've been up all night, baby
Leanin' on the windowsill
Well, if I die
On top of the hill
And if I don't make it
You know my baby will

Don't the moon look good, mama
Shinin' through the trees?
Don't the brakeman look good, mama
Flagging down the "Double E"?
Don't the sun look good
Goin' down over the sea?
Don't my gal look fine
When she's comin' after me?

Now the wintertime is coming
The windows are filled with frost
I went to tell everybody
But I could not get across
Well, I wanna be your lover, baby
I don't wanna be your boss
Don't say I never warned you
When your train gets lost

来自别克 6

我有个看墓园的女人，你知道她帮我带娃
但我深情的妈妈啊，你知道她还帮我藏身
她是个垃圾场天使，她总给我面包
唉若我快死了，你知道她准会为我盖上毯子

好啦，当油管破裂，当我在跨河大桥上迷路
当我在高速公路或水边分崩离析
她奔下高速准备用线头把我缝起
唉若我快死了，你知道她准会为我盖上毯子

好啦，她不会让我紧张，她不是话痨
她走起路来活像博·迪德利[1]，不需要拐杖
她总是给这把 410 枪上满子弹
唉若我快死了，你知道她准会为我盖上毯子

好啦妈妈，你知道我要一台蒸汽挖土机刨掉死尸
我需要一辆自卸卡车，妈妈，来卸下我的脑袋

---

1. 博·迪德利（Bo Diddley，1928—2008），美国节奏蓝调、摇滚歌手，在蓝调向摇滚乐的转变中起了重要作用。

她带给我所有，甚至更多，正如我所说
唉若我快死了，你知道她准会为我盖上毯子

From a Buick 6

I got this graveyard woman, you know she keeps my kid
But my soulful mama, you know she keeps me hid
She's a junkyard angel and she always gives me bread
Well, if I go down dyin', you know she bound to put a
blanket on my bed

Well, when the pipeline gets broken and I'm lost on the
river bridge
I'm cracked up on the highway and on the water's edge
She comes down the thruway ready to sew me up with
thread
Well, if I go down dyin', you know she bound to put a
blanket on my bed

Well, she don't make me nervous, she don't talk too much
She walks like Bo Diddley and she don't need no crutch
She keeps this four-ten all loaded with lead
Well, if I go down dyin', you know she bound to put a
blanket on my bed

Well, you know I need a steam shovel mama to keep away
the dead
I need a dump truck mama to unload my head
She brings me everything and more, and just like I said
Well, if I go down dyin', you know she bound to put a
blanket on my bed

瘦男人歌谣

你走进房间
手里握着铅笔
你看见一个赤膊汉
你问：“那是谁？”
你那么拼
却不知道
回家以后
该说啥

因为这儿正有事发生
你却一头雾水
不是吗，琼斯先生？

你抬起脑袋
问道：“就是这儿？”
有人指着你说
“这是他的”
你说：“啥是我的？”
另一个人说：“有啥是呢？”
你说：“哦上帝

难道这儿只有我一个？”

因为这儿正有事发生
你却一头雾水
不是吗，琼斯先生？

你出示门票
去看怪胎秀
怪胎一听你说话
就径直向你走
他说：“做个畸形人
感觉怎么样？”
你说：“难以忍受”
当他递给你一根骨头

因为这儿正有事发生
你却一头雾水
不是吗，琼斯先生？

你在伐木工人群里
有不少眼线
每当有人攻击你的想象力
他们就提供信息

但根本没人表示尊敬
反正他们不过指望你
开张支票
给能减税的慈善机构

你跟教授们交往过
他们都爱你仪表堂堂
你和杰出的律师讨论过
麻风病人和骗子
你读完了 F. S. 菲茨杰拉德
所有的书
你饱览万卷
全世界都知道

因为这儿正有事发生
你却一头雾水
不是吗，琼斯先生？

好了，吞剑人也朝你走来
他跪下来
画个十字
敲响高鞋跟
冷不丁地

他问你感觉怎么样
他还说：“你的嗓子，还你了
谢谢你借我”

因为这儿正有事发生
你却一头雾水
不是吗，琼斯先生？

现在你看见独眼的侏儒
大声叫出“**现在**”这个词
你说：“这是要干吗？”
他说：“哈？”
你说：“这什么意思？”
他回叫：“你这头母牛
给我点牛奶
要不就滚回家”

因为这儿正有事发生
你却一头雾水
不是吗，琼斯先生？

好了，你走进房间
像头骆驼，你皱眉

把眼珠放进口袋
把鼻子伏在地上
真该立个法
禁止你乱晃
你该被勒令
把耳机套上

因为这儿正有事发生
你却一头雾水
不是吗，琼斯先生？

Ballad of a Thin Man

You walk into the room
With your pencil in your hand
You see somebody naked
And you say, "Who is that man?"
You try so hard
But you don't understand
Just what you'll say
When you get home

Because something is happening here
But you don't know what it is
Do you, Mister Jones?

You raise up your head
And you ask, "Is this where it is?"
And somebody points to you and says
"It's his"
And you say, "What's mine?"
And somebody else says, "Where what is?"
And you say, "Oh my God
Am I here all alone?"

Because something is happening here
But you don't know what it is
Do you, Mister Jones?

You hand in your ticket
And you go watch the geek
Who immediately walks up to you

When he hears you speak
And says, "How does it feel
To be such a freak?"
And you say, "Impossible"
As he hands you a bone

Because something is happening here
But you don't know what it is
Do you, Mister Jones?

You have many contacts
Among the lumberjacks
To get you facts
When someone attacks your imagination
But nobody has any respect
Anyway they already expect you
To just give a check
To tax-deductible charity organizations

You've been with the professors
And they've all liked your looks
With great lawyers you have
Discussed lepers and crooks
You've been through all of
F. Scott Fitzgerald's books
You're very well read
It's well known

Because something is happening here
But you don't know what it is
Do you, Mister Jones?

Well, the sword swallower, he comes up to you

And then he kneels
He crosses himself
And then he clicks his high heels
And without further notice
He asks you how it feels
And he says, "Here is your throat back
Thanks for the loan"

Because something is happening here
But you don't know what it is
Do you, Mister Jones?

Now you see this one-eyed midget
Shouting the word "NOW"
And you say, "For what reason?"
And he says, "How?"
And you say, "What does this mean?"
And he screams back, "You're a cow
Give me some milk
Or else go home"

Because something is happening here
But you don't know what it is
Do you, Mister Jones?

Well, you walk into the room
Like a camel and then you frown
You put your eyes in your pocket
And your nose on the ground
There ought to be a law
Against you comin' around
You should be made
To wear earphones

Because something is happening here
But you don't know what it is
Do you, Mister Jones?

准女王简[1]

当你母亲退回你所有的请柬
当你父亲对你的姐姐抱怨
说你厌倦了自己，厌倦了自己的造物
你会来看我吗，简女王？
你会来看我吗，简女王？

当所有卖花女都索回她们借出的东西
当她们的玫瑰芬芳已烟消云散
当你所有的孩子都开始恨你
你会来看我吗，简女王？
你会来看我吗，简女王？

如今当你雇过的所有小丑
都战死沙场或死得轻如鸿毛
当你腻烦了所有这些周而复始
你会来看我吗，简女王？

---

1. 简·格雷（Lady Jane Grey，1536/1537—1554），英国贵族，亨利八世的曾外孙女。在位只有九日，且其继位违反议会法令，后被废黜，一般不正式算作英国女王。

你会来看我吗，简女王？

当你所有的顾问都在你脚下
手舞足蹈，要说服你相信自己的痛苦
要证明你的结论应该更加激进
你会来看我吗，简女王？
你会来看我吗，简女王？

如今当所有你曾以德报怨的匪徒
扯下面巾，开始发牢骚
当你渴望一个不必同他讲话的人
你会来看我吗，简女王？
你会来看我吗，简女王？

Queen Jane Approximately

When your mother sends back all your invitations
And your father to your sister he explains
That you're tired of yourself and all of your creations
Won't you come see me, Queen Jane?
Won't you come see me, Queen Jane?

Now when all of the flower ladies want back what they have
lent you
And the smell of their roses does not remain
And all of your children start to resent you
Won't you come see me, Queen Jane?
Won't you come see me, Queen Jane?

Now when all the clowns that you have commissioned
Have died in battle or in vain
And you're sick of all this repetition
Won't you come see me, Queen Jane?
Won't you come see me, Queen Jane?

When all of your advisers heave their plastic
At your feet to convince you of your pain
Trying to prove that your conclusions should be more
drastic
Won't you come see me, Queen Jane?
Won't you come see me, Queen Jane?

Now when all the bandits that you turned your other cheek to
All lay down their bandanas and complain
And you want somebody you don't have to speak to

Won't you come see me, Queen Jane?
Won't you come see me, Queen Jane?

重访 61 号公路

噢，上帝对亚伯拉罕说：“宰个儿子给我”[1]
老亚伯说：“大哥，你准是在耍我”
上帝说：“没。”亚伯说：“啥？”
上帝说：“亚伯啊，你想怎么着都成
但下次碰到我，你最好撒丫子跑”
于是亚伯说：“你想在哪宰？”
上帝说：“去 61 号公路”

佐治亚·山姆爱流鼻血
社保署不肯给他衣服
他问穷鬼霍华德，我能去哪
老霍说据我所知只有一处
山姆说快快告诉我，赶路呢
老霍华德拿枪一指：
那边，沿着 61 号公路

指头麦克对路易王说

1.《旧约·创世记》22，上帝试验亚伯拉罕，谕其带一子燔祭。又，迪伦父亲名亚伯兰（Abram）。

我有四十条红的白的蓝的鞋带
还有一千台哑巴电话机
你说说我上哪处理掉这些玩意
路易王说孩子啊容我想想
然后说好叻我觉得这都不是事
你就统统拿去 61 号公路

这会儿第五个闺女在第十二夜[1]
告诉第一个爹：出事了
她说我的肤色白过了头
他说来来站到光里，嗯说得没错
让我去告诉二妈，这事已办妥
可是二妈正跟第七个儿子一起
两个都在 61 号公路上

这会儿浪荡的赌棍穷极无聊
想整出下一次世界大战
他找到一个差点摔趴的赞助商
他说我以前没搞过这个

---

1. 第十二夜，主显节前夕。自 12 月 25 日的圣诞夜起算，第十二夜过后即主显节，以志东方三博士对耶稣基督的朝拜。美国新奥尔良又将第十二夜视为狂欢节之始。此处亦指涉莎士比亚同名戏剧。

但我觉得吧这都不是事
咱们只消在日头下摆几排露天座
就在 61 号公路上

Highway 61 Revisited

Oh God said to Abraham, "Kill me a son"
Abe says, "Man, you must be puttin' me on"
God say, "No." Abe say, "What?"
God say, "You can do what you want Abe, but
The next time you see me comin' you better run"
Well Abe says, "Where do you want this killin' done?"
God says, "Out on Highway 61"

Well Georgia Sam he had a bloody nose
Welfare Department they wouldn't give him no clothes
He asked poor Howard where can I go
Howard said there's only one place I know
Sam said tell me quick man I got to run
Ol' Howard just pointed with his gun
And said that way down on Highway 61

Well Mack the Finger said to Louie the King
I got forty red white and blue shoestrings
And a thousand telephones that don't ring
Do you know where I can get rid of these things
And Louie the King said let me think for a minute son
And he said yes I think it can be easily done
Just take everything down to Highway 61

Now the fifth daughter on the twelfth night
Told the first father that things weren't right
My complexion she said is much too white
He said come here and step into the light he says hmm
  you're right

Let me tell the second mother this has been done
But the second mother was with the seventh son
And they were both out on Highway 61

Now the rovin' gambler he was very bored
He was tryin' to create a next world war
He found a promoter who nearly fell off the floor
He said I never engaged in this kind of thing before
But yes I think it can be very easily done
We'll just put some bleachers out in the sun
And have it on Highway 61

恰似大拇指汤姆[1]蓝调

你在华雷斯的雨中迷路时
正值复活节
你又失着重
悲观也不能帮你过关
别摆架子咯
当你走在莫格街大道
那儿有几个饥肠辘辘的女人
着实把你狠揍一通

现在若你看到圣安妮[2]
请代我向她致谢
我动弹不得
手指全打了结
我没有力气
爬起来再战一回
而且我最好的朋友，我的医生
甚至不肯说出我得了啥病

---

1. 大拇指汤姆，英国民间童话中如父亲拇指般高的小男孩。
2. 圣安妮，在《圣经》不见提及，但传统上被认定为圣母马利亚之母。

甜心梅琳达
农夫们管她叫作忧郁女神
她英语说得呱呱叫
她请你上她屋里去
而你那么好心
注意没有去太早
于是她取走你的嗓音
留下你对着月亮咆哮

在“安居计划山坡”[1]上
不是财富就是名望
两者你必须选一样
虽然两样都名不副实
若你看上去快要变傻了
最好赶紧原路滚回
因为条子不需要你
也希望你不需要他们

如今所有的权威名流
只会干站着吹牛逼

1.“安居计划山坡”，引自杰克·凯鲁亚克的小说《荒凉天使》（*Desolation Angels*）中的地名。

吹嘘自己如何敲诈警卫官
逼他离开岗位
并且顺路接上
刚从海边抵达的天使
天使起先美貌无比
离开时却恍如幽灵

我开始痛饮勃艮第酒
但很快碰到了大麻烦
所有人都说事儿变糟时
他们会在背后挺我
可当我成了笑柄
连个逼我摊牌的人都没剩下
我要回纽约城去了
我想我已经受够了

Just Like Tom Thumb's Blues

When you're lost in the rain in Juarez
And it's Eastertime too
And your gravity fails
And negativity don't pull you through
Don't put on any airs
When you're down on Rue Morgue Avenue
They got some hungry women there
And they really make a mess outa you

Now if you see Saint Annie
Please tell her thanks a lot
I cannot move
My fingers are all in a knot
I don't have the strength
To get up and take another shot
And my best friend, my doctor
Won't even say what it is I've got

Sweet Melinda
The peasants call her the goddess of gloom
She speaks good English
And she invites you up into her room
And you're so kind
And careful not to go to her too soon
And she takes your voice
And leaves you howling at the moon

Up on Housing Project Hill
It's either fortune or fame

You must pick up one or the other
Though neither of them are to be what they claim
If you're lookin' to get silly
You better go back to from where you came
Because the cops don't need you
And man they expect the same

Now all the authorities
They just stand around and boast
How they blackmailed the sergeant-at-arms
Into leaving his post
And picking up Angel who
Just arrived here from the coast
Who looked so fine at first
But left looking just like a ghost

I started out on burgundy
But soon hit the harder stuff
Everybody said they'd stand behind me
When the game got rough
But the joke was on me
There was nobody even there to call my bluff
I'm going back to New York City
I do believe I've had enough

荒芜巷[1]

他们在兜售绞刑明信片[2]
他们正把护照涂棕[3]
美容院里挤满水手
马戏团已进城
瞎长官已来到
他们让他陷入迷狂
一只手绑在走钢丝人身上
另一只插进裤袋
防暴小分队焦躁不安
他们需要有个地方去
当今晚我同女士向外张望
从荒芜巷

灰姑娘看起来那么随和

---

1. 源自凯鲁亚克的小说名字《荒凉天使》，以及斯坦贝克的小说《罐头厂街》（*Cannery Row*）。

2.1920 年 6 月 15 日，在迪伦的故乡明尼苏达州德卢斯，有三名在马戏团工作的黑人，涉嫌强奸白人少女，遭民众私下绞死，行刑现场的照片被印制成明信片出售。

3. 美国行政官员因公护照为棕红色。

“总得有人主动。”她微笑着
把手插进屁股口袋
颇有贝蒂·戴维斯[1]之风
罗密欧走进来，呻吟着
“我相信你属于我”
有人说：“伙计你来错了地方
最好赶紧走”
救护车开走后
仅剩的声音
就是灰姑娘正挥帚
在荒芜巷

现在月亮几乎隐没
星星开始捉迷藏
连算命女士
都收起了她全部的家当
所有人，除了该隐和亚伯
还有巴黎圣母院的驼子
每个人都在做爱

---

1. 贝蒂·戴维斯（Bette Davis，1908—1989），美国演员，获得十次奥斯卡最佳女主角提名。她把手插在后兜的造型见于《化石森林》（*The Petrified Forest*，1936）等片中。

要不就在盼望一场雨
那个好撒玛利亚人，他正穿衣
他正为演出做准备
他今晚要去嘉年华
就在荒芜巷

现在，奥菲莉娅[1]在窗下
我为她担惊受怕
在二十二岁生日那天
她已是个老姑娘
对她而言，死亡无比浪漫
她穿一件铁马甲
投身宗教是她的职业
了无生气是她的罪业
尽管双眼紧盯着
挪亚宏伟的彩虹[2]
日复一日她却窥视着
荒芜巷深处

爱因斯坦假扮罗宾汉

---

1. 奥菲莉娅，莎士比亚的戏剧《哈姆雷特》中哈姆雷特的未婚妻，因疯癫溺水而死。
2.《旧约 · 创世记》9，上帝以彩虹为记，与挪亚立约不再发大洪水毁灭世界。

把记忆放进箱子
一小时前从这儿走过
和一个朋友，一个嫉妒的僧侣
当他讨一根香烟
看起来可真叫心惊肉跳
然后他边走边嗅着排水管道
一路背着字母表
如今你根本不会想正眼看他
但老早以前他就名闻遐迩
拉着他的电子小提琴
在荒芜巷

污秽博士把自己的世界
保存在一只皮革杯中
但他所有无性的病人
都想把它炸飞
现在他的护士，一个本地的失意者
她负责看管氰化物毒气房
她还要保管那些纸牌
上面写着："垂怜他的灵魂"
他们都吹六孔哨笛
你可以听见他们的演奏
假如你把脖子伸得足够长

从荒芜巷

马路对面他们钉死了窗帘
他们正准备庆祝欢宴
剧院魅影[1]是一位
神父的完美画像
他们用勺子喂食卡萨诺瓦[2]
要让他更安心点
接着他们将用自信杀死他
在用词语给他下毒后
魅影对瘦骨嶙峋的姑娘尖叫
“滚出去，难道你们不知道
卡萨诺瓦正接受体罚，因为他
去了荒芜巷”

正是半夜，所有特工
所有超人，全体出动
把一切知道得比他们多的人
统统聚拢

---

1. 剧院魅影，法国推理小说家加斯东·勒鲁（Gaston Leroux）的同名作品，后经安德鲁·韦伯（Andrew Lloyd Webber）改编成音乐剧而闻名。
2. 贾科莫·卡萨诺瓦（Giacomo Casanova，1725—1798），意大利冒险家、作家，有“情圣”之称。

然后把他们带到工厂
在那儿把心脏病器械
绑在他们肩头
接着从城堡里
运来煤油，运输者
是保险业务员，他们
出去巡街，确保没有人
逃去荒芜巷

荣耀归于尼禄的海王星
泰坦尼克号起航在黎明
所有人都嚷嚷着
“你站在谁那边？”
埃兹拉·庞德和 T. S. 艾略特
在船长塔里斗殴
卡利普索女歌手讥笑他们
渔民手拿花束
在大海的窗户间
妩媚的美人鱼在那儿漂游
没人需要想太多
关于荒芜巷

是的，昨天我收到了你的信

（大概是在门把坏掉的时候）
你问我过得怎么样
这是在开玩笑吧？
所有你提到的那些人
没错，我都认识，尽是怂货
我得重新组装他们的脸
再给他们重新起名
此刻我没法好好阅读
别再给我寄信了，别
除非你寄出的信件
来自荒芜巷

Desolation Row

They're selling postcards of the hanging
They're painting the passports brown
The beauty parlor is filled with sailors
The circus is in town
Here comes the blind commissioner
They've got him in a trance
One hand is tied to the tight-rope walker
The other is in his pants
And the riot squad they're restless
They need somewhere to go
As Lady and I look out tonight
From Desolation Row

Cinderella, she seems so easy
"It takes one to know one," she smiles
And puts her hands in her back pockets
Bette Davis style
And in comes Romeo, he's moaning
"You Belong to Me I Believe"
And someone says, "You're in the wrong place my friend
You better leave"
And the only sound that's left
After the ambulances go
Is Cinderella sweeping up
On Desolation Row

Now the moon is almost hidden
The stars are beginning to hide
The fortune-telling lady

Has even taken all her things inside
All except for Cain and Abel
And the hunchback of Notre Dame
Everybody is making love
Or else expecting rain
And the Good Samaritan, he's dressing
He's getting ready for the show
He's going to the carnival tonight
On Desolation Row

Now Ophelia, she's 'neath the window
For her I feel so afraid
On her twenty-second birthday
She already is an old maid
To her, death is quite romantic
She wears an iron vest
Her profession's her religion
Her sin is her lifelessness
And though her eyes are fixed upon
Noah's great rainbow
She spends her time peeking
Into Desolation Row

Einstein, disguised as Robin Hood
With his memories in a trunk
Passed this way an hour ago
With his friend, a jealous monk
He looked so immaculately frightful
As he bummed a cigarette
Then he went off sniffing drainpipes
And reciting the alphabet
Now you would not think to look at him
But he was famous long ago

For playing the electric violin
On Desolation Row

Dr. Filth, he keeps his world
Inside of a leather cup
But all his sexless patients
They're trying to blow it up
Now his nurse, some local loser
She's in charge of the cyanide hole
And she also keeps the cards that read
"Have Mercy on His Soul"
They all play on pennywhistles
You can hear them blow
If you lean your head out far enough
From Desolation Row

Across the street they've nailed the curtains
They're getting ready for the feast
The Phantom of the Opera
A perfect image of a priest
They're spoonfeeding Casanova
To get him to feel more assured
Then they'll kill him with self-confidence
After poisoning him with words
And the Phantom's shouting to skinny girls
"Get Outa Here If You Don't Know
Casanova is just being punished for going
To Desolation Row"

Now at midnight all the agents
And the superhuman crew
Come out and round up everyone
That knows more than they do

Then they bring them to the factory
Where the heart-attack machine
Is strapped across their shoulders
And then the kerosene
Is brought down from the castles
By insurance men who go
Check to see that nobody is escaping
To Desolation Row

Praise be to Nero's Neptune
The Titanic sails at dawn
And everybody's shouting
"Which Side Are You On?"
And Ezra Pound and T. S. Eliot
Fighting in the captain's tower
While calypso singers laugh at them
And fishermen hold flowers
Between the windows of the sea
Where lovely mermaids flow
And nobody has to think too much
About Desolation Row

Yes, I received your letter yesterday
(About the time the doorknob broke)
When you asked how I was doing
Was that some kind of joke?
All these people that you mention
Yes, I know them, they're quite lame
I had to rearrange their faces
And give them all another name
Right now I can't read too good
Don't send me no more letters no
Not unless you mail them
From Desolation Row

准是第四街[1]

你胆子真大
说你是我朋友
我倒霉那会
你不过咧嘴旁观

你胆子真大
说你乐于助人
你不过想站在
胜者的阵营

你说我让你失望
你知道不是那样
如果你当真被伤得深
干吗不尽情表露

你说你失去了信仰
但事实不是这样
你没有信仰可失去

---

1. 迪伦在 20 世纪 60 年代初，曾住在纽约第四街。

而且你心知肚明

我知道为什么
你在背后嚼我舌头
我曾属于你如今
混迹的人群

你以为我傻吗
以为我会交往那个人
他试图藏匿
他本来就一无所知的东西

你在街头撞见我
你总是假装惊奇
你说："还好吗？""祝好运"
你压根心口不一

等你知道得和我一样多
你宁肯看到我瘫痪
干吗不直接跳出来一次
大声叫出来？

不，我感觉并不好

看见你拥抱那些心碎时
如果我是一名神偷
或许就会抢走它们

现在我知道你不满于
你的职位，你的立场
你难道就不明白
这跟我无关

我希望哪怕就一次
你能穿上我的鞋
哪怕只有那一刻
让我成为你

是的，我希望哪怕就一次
你我能对调身份
你就会知道，看见你
是怎样腻味透顶的事

Positively 4th Street

You got a lotta nerve
To say you are my friend
When I was down
You just stood there grinning

You got a lotta nerve
To say you got a helping hand to lend
You just want to be on
The side that's winning

You say I let you down
You know it's not like that
If you're so hurt
Why then don't you show it

You say you lost your faith
But that's not where it's at
You had no faith to lose
And you know it

I know the reason
That you talk behind my back
I used to be among the crowd
You're in with

Do you take me for such a fool
To think I'd make contact
With the one who tries to hide
What he don't know to begin with

You see me on the street
You always act surprised
You say, "How are you?" "Good luck"
But you don't mean it

When you know as well as me
You'd rather see me paralyzed
Why don't you just come out once
And scream it

No, I do not feel that good
When I see the heartbreaks you embrace
If I was a master thief
Perhaps I'd rob them

And now I know you're dissatisfied
With your position and your place
Don't you understand
It's not my problem

I wish that for just one time
You could stand inside my shoes
And just for that one moment
I could be you

Yes, I wish that for just one time
You could stand inside my shoes
You'd know what a drag it is
To see you

你能不能从窗口爬出去?

他坐在你的房间，他的墓穴，满腹诡计
除了复仇没有其他念头
诅咒不能回话的死者
我肯定他并无意
朝你看，除非是说
他需要你，去试验他的意图

你能不能从窗口爬出去?
动动手臂和腿不会毁了你
你怎么能说他阴魂不散?
你可以随时回去他身边

他看起来那么真诚，这就是他的感受?
当他试图剥下月亮的皮，袒露它
用生意人的怒火，用跪姿寻血犬?
如果他需要第三只眼，只需长出来
他只需你开口，或给他递支粉笔
或在他扔掉粉笔后帮他捡起来

你能不能从窗口爬出去?

动动手臂和腿不会毁了你
你怎么能说他阴魂不散?
你可以随时回去他身边

他为何看起来那么大义凛然，当你神色骤变
你就那么害怕，那只用来囚禁他的箱子
他那帮种族屠杀的蠢货和狐朋狗友
重建关于小小锡女的信仰
那能支持他们的立场，但你的脸淤肿不堪
出来吧，夜幕正拉开——

你能不能从窗口爬出去?
动动手臂和腿不会毁了你
你怎么能说他阴魂不散?
你可以随时回去他身边

Can You Please Crawl Out Your Window?

He sits in your room, his tomb, with a fist full of tacks
Preoccupied with his vengeance
Cursing the dead that can't answer him back
I'm sure that he has no intentions
Of looking your way, unless it's to say
That he needs you to test his inventions

Can you please crawl out your window?
Use your arms and legs it won't ruin you
How can you say he will haunt you?
You can go back to him any time you want to

He looks so truthful, is this how he feels
Trying to peel the moon and expose it
With his businesslike anger and his bloodhounds that kneel
If he needs a third eye he just grows it
He just needs you to talk or to hand him his chalk
Or pick it up after he throws it

Can you please crawl out your window?
Use your arms and legs it won't ruin you
How can you say he will haunt you?
You can go back to him any time you want to

Why does he look so righteous while your face is so changed
Are you frightened of the box you keep him in
While his genocide fools and his friends rearrange
Their religion of the little tin women
That backs up their views but your face is so bruised

Come on out the dark is beginning

Can you please crawl out your window?
Use your arms and legs it won't ruin you
How can you say he will haunt you?
You can go back to him any time you want to

坐在带刺铁丝篱上

我花了一千五百万十二块七毛二
我花了一千两百二十七块五毛五
观看我的猎犬咬兔子
看我的足球坐在带刺铁丝篱上

好了，我脾气上来了，脚步迈不快
是啊，我脾气上来了脚步迈不快
好了，这阿拉伯医生走进来给我打一针
但不肯告诉我这病到底能不能好

好了，我拥有这女人，她对我步步紧逼
是啊，这个我的女人，用蜂房让我疯狂
她正管我叫斯坦
或者叫我克莱夫先生

当然啦，你会觉得这歌是即兴重复段
我知道，你会觉得这歌是峭壁一块
除非你曾经钻进隧道
并从带刺铁丝篱上坠落 69 或 70 英尺

——通宵达旦！

Sitting on a Barbed-Wire Fence

I paid fifteen million dollars, twelve hundred and seventy-
  two cents
I paid one thousand two hundred twenty-seven dollars and
  fifty-five cents
See my hound dog bite a rabbit
And my football's sittin' on a barbed-wire fence

Well, my temperature rises and my feet don't walk so fast
Yes, my temperature rises and my feet don't walk so fast
Well, this Arabian doctor came in, gave me a shot
But wouldn't tell me if what I had would last

Well, this woman I've got, she's filling me with her drive
Yes, this woman I've got, she's thrillin' me with her hive
She's calling me Stan
Or else she calls me Mister Clive

Of course, you're gonna think this song is a riff
I know you're gonna think this song is a cliff
Unless you've been inside a tunnel
And fell down 69, 70 feet over a barbed-wire fence

All night!

2. i got 14 fevers/ i got 5 believers...dressed up like men
tell your mama not to worry/

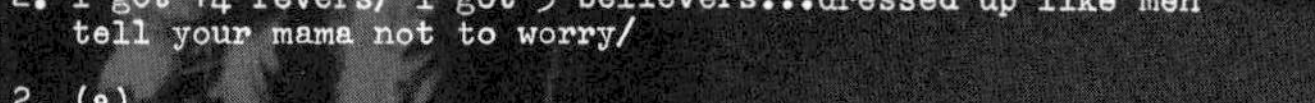

2. (a) tell your mama & your pappa i'm trying to keep from dying to

3. tell your mama & your pappa that there's nothing wrong with my
jugler vein

tell your mama i love her & tell your sister Alice the same

Lonely Lonely miss

4. (comes from) (ing)
when you sleep on windows & you stay up all nite swallowing rocks

making love to / making love to

5.
i shoulda sent her to Hong Kong stead of leaving

金发叠金发

Blonde on Blonde

马世芳 译

李皖 译（郝佳 校）

从 1965 年到 1966 年短短十三个月，鲍勃 · 迪伦连发三张旷世经典：1965 年的《全数带回家》和《重访 61 号公路》，及“三部曲”的压轴《金发叠金发》。这三张专辑将民谣和摇滚两条大河汇流一处，是影响乐史至巨的“井喷”事件。

1965 年 10 月，鲍勃 · 迪伦在纽约开始筹备新专辑，录了几首歌都不满意，最后留用的只有《我们总有一个人要明白（迟早的事）》一首。次年 2 月，他从纽约远赴“乡村音乐之都”——田纳西州的纳什维尔，在文化气质截然不同的环境，和一群当地顶尖“棚虫”乐手合作，以近乎即兴的方式创造出专辑中的十几首歌曲。

与前两张专辑相比，《金发叠金发》的音乐不再能量外显、气场分明，也不再能够清楚分辨“民谣”和“摇滚”两种编曲方向。鲍勃 · 迪伦曾在 1978 年的访谈中提及《金发叠金发》是最接近他心目中理想的声音：“那是一种纤薄、狂野的水银样的声音，金属闪耀的黄金色，连带着它召唤出来的一切。”

专辑的歌词，仍然充满超现实的意象、奇幻的人物、警世的格言，更多了许多破碎扭曲的爱情风景。前两张专辑那些愤世、乖张、梦魇式的末日寓言，在这儿往往掉转过来，探往内观的、私我的世界。

《金发叠金发》是两张一套的“双专辑”，全长七十三分钟。这是摇滚史的创举，为后继者示范了这种宏大的规格。1966 年，摇滚正在演化成为一门足以承载思想与技艺的创作形式，准备迈入第一个烂熟的黄金时期，《金发叠金发》便是其中最早矗起的一尊丰碑。

本专辑中的附加歌词由李皖先生翻译、郝佳先生校，其余数首由本人翻译。

马世芳

雨天女人十二与三十五号

他们拿石头砸昏你趁你想努力变好
他们拿石头砸昏你就像之前讲的那么搞
他们拿石头砸昏你趁你想回家
他们拿石头砸昏你趁你正寂寞
可我并不觉得多孤单
反正人人都得被砸翻[1]

他们拿石头砸昏你趁你在街上
他们拿石头砸昏你趁你想占座不让
他们拿石头砸昏你趁你来回走
他们拿石头砸昏你趁你去门口
可我并不觉得多孤单
反正人人都得被砸翻

他们拿石头砸昏你趁你吃着早餐
他们拿石头砸昏你趁你年轻有为
他们拿石头砸昏你趁你努力挣钱
他们拿石头砸昏你然后说："一路顺风"

---

1. 砸昏、砸翻，有"用石头砸死"与"嗑药嗑上头"的双关义。

告诉你，我可不觉得孤单
反正人人都得被砸翻

他们拿石头砸昏你然后说这就完事
他们拿石头砸昏你然后回来再干一次
他们拿石头砸昏你趁你开着车
他们拿石头砸昏你趁你弹吉他
可我并不觉得多孤单
反正人人都得被砸翻

他们拿石头砸昏你趁你独自漫步
他们拿石头砸昏你趁你走回家门口
他们拿石头砸昏你然后说你好勇敢
他们拿石头砸昏你趁你进坟墓
可我并不觉得多孤单
反正人人都得被砸翻

Rainy Day Women #12 & 35

Well, they'll stone ya when you're trying to be so good
They'll stone ya just a-like they said they would
They'll stone ya when you're tryin' to go home
Then they'll stone ya when you're there all alone
But I would not feel so all alone
Everybody must get stoned

Well, they'll stone ya when you're walkin' 'long the street
They'll stone ya when you're tryin' to keep your seat
They'll stone ya when you're walkin' on the floor
They'll stone ya when you're walkin' to the door
But I would not feel so all alone
Everybody must get stoned

They'll stone ya when you're at the breakfast table
They'll stone ya when you are young and able
They'll stone ya when you're tryin' to make a buck
They'll stone ya and then they'll say, "good luck"
Tell ya what, I would not feel so all alone
Everybody must get stoned

Well, they'll stone you and say that it's the end
Then they'll stone you and then they'll come back again
They'll stone you when you're riding in your car
They'll stone you when you're playing your guitar
Yes, but I would not feel so all alone
Everybody must get stoned

Well, they'll stone you when you walk all alone

They'll stone you when you are walking home
They'll stone you and then say you are brave
They'll stone you when you are set down in your grave
But I would not feel so all alone
Everybody must get stoned

抵押我的时间

嘿，一大清早
直到半夜
我头痛像中毒
可是感觉挺舒服
我把时间抵押给你
希望你也能来我这里[1]

嘿，流浪汉跳起来
又自自然然地下来
偷偷带走我的宝贝
又想把我也偷走
我把时间抵押给你
希望你也能来我这里

何不跟着我，宝贝
想去哪里，我带你走
万一实在没搞头
最先知道的也是你

---

1. 来我这里，也有“渡过难关”“脱险”之意。

我把时间抵押给你
希望你也能来我这里

嘿，房间太挤
我简直不能呼吸
大家都走光，只剩我和你
而我不能最后才撤离
我把时间抵押给你
希望你也能来我这里

嘿，他们叫了救护车
于是就来了一辆
某人真是好运气
不过是意外一场
我把时间抵押给你
希望你也能来我这里

Pledging My Time

Well, early in the mornin'
'Til late at night
I got a poison headache
But I feel all right
I'm pledging my time to you
Hopin' you'll come through, too

Well, the hobo jumped up
He came down natur'lly
After he stole my baby
Then he wanted to steal me
But I'm pledging my time to you
Hopin' you'll come through, too

Won't you come with me, baby?
I'll take you where you wanna go
And if it don't work out
You'll be the first to know
I'm pledging my time to you
Hopin' you'll come through, too

Well, the room is so stuffy
I can hardly breathe
Ev'rybody's gone but me and you
And I can't be the last to leave
I'm pledging my time to you
Hopin' you'll come through, too

Well, they sent for the ambulance

And one was sent
Somebody got lucky
But it was an accident
Now I'm pledging my time to you
Hopin' you'll come through, too

乔安娜的幻象

不就是这么一个要作弄人的夜晚？当你只想好好安静下来
我们困坐在这里，却又尽力掩饰
路易丝捧着一掌雨水，挑逗你，看你能否抗拒
对面阁楼灯火闪烁
房间里暖气管轻声咳嗽
乡村电台歌声正温柔
然而没有什么该关掉，真的没有
只有路易丝和她的情人，如此缠绵
而乔安娜的幻象，占据了我的脑海

空地里，女士们拿一串钥匙玩捉迷藏
彻夜不归的女孩，悄悄说着远方D线地铁的大冒险
我们听得见守夜人把手电筒开了又关
自问到底是我还是她们已经疯癫？
路易丝，她很好，她就在身边
如此脆弱，看上去像一面镜子
却也让这一切清楚明白：
乔安娜并不在此
电气的鬼魂在她脸骨嚎叫
如今乔安娜的幻象，取代了我的所在

小男孩迷了路，他太把自己当回事
他吹嘘自己的不幸，喜欢活得危机四伏
提到她的名字
他对我说起一次吻别
这人确实胆大包天，如此一无是处
向墙壁碎嘴牢骚，而我人在门厅
啊，怎么可能解释明白？
说下去，竟是如此艰难
而乔安娜的幻象，让我长夜独醒，直到天明

在博物馆，永恒升堂受审
众声回荡：所谓救赎，没多久一定变成这样
然而蒙娜丽莎一定怀着公路的悲歌
你一眼就懂，凭她微笑的模样
看远古壁花纷纷凝结
果冻脸女人喷嚏连连
听那长胡子的说："天啊
我找不到膝盖啦"
啊，珠宝和双筒望远镜悬垂在骡子的头颅
但乔安娜的幻象，让这一切显得如此残酷

小贩对假意关心自己的伯爵夫人开口：
"说说谁不是寄生虫，我就出去为他祈祷"

但就像路易丝常说的
“你看不了太多，不是吗？”
同时她亲自为他做了准备
圣母依旧没有出现
眼看着空荡荡的牢笼已经腐朽
她上台的披风曾在其中翻涌
提琴手踏上旅途
他写：“每件欠下的，如今悉数还清”
在载鱼的货车后部
我的良知猛然爆炸
口琴纷纷奏起，那是万能的钥匙[1]，还有雨水
如今乔安娜的幻象，便是仅剩的一切

1. 万能的钥匙，亦可直译为“骷髅的曲调”。

Visions of Johanna

Ain't it just like the night to play tricks when you're trying
to be so quiet?
We sit here stranded, though we're all doin' our best to
deny it
And Louise holds a handful of rain, temptin' you to defy it
Lights flicker from the opposite loft
In this room the heat pipes just cough
The country music station plays soft
But there's nothing, really nothing to turn off
Just Louise and her lover so entwined
And these visions of Johanna that conquer my mind

In the empty lot where the ladies play blindman's bluff with
the key chain
And the all-night girls they whisper of escapades out on the
"D" train
We can hear the night watchman click his flashlight
Ask himself if it's him or them that's really insane
Louise, she's all right, she's just near
She's delicate and seems like the mirror
But she just makes it all too concise and too clear
That Johanna's not here
The ghost of 'lectricity howls in the bones of her face
Where these visions of Johanna have now taken my place

Now, little boy lost, he takes himself so seriously
He brags of his misery, he likes to live dangerously
And when bringing her name up
He speaks of a farewell kiss to me

He's sure got a lotta gall to be so useless and all
Muttering small talk at the wall while I'm in the hall
How can I explain?
Oh, it's so hard to get on
And these visions of Johanna, they kept me up past the
dawn

Inside the museums, Infinity goes up on trial
Voices echo this is what salvation must be like after a while
But Mona Lisa musta had the highway blues
You can tell by the way she smiles
See the primitive wallflower freeze
When the jelly-faced women all sneeze
Hear the one with the mustache say, "Jeeze
I can't find my knees"
Oh, jewels and binoculars hang from the head of the mule
But these visions of Johanna, they make it all seem so cruel

The peddler now speaks to the countess who's pretending to
care for him
Sayin', "Name me someone that's not a parasite and I'll go
out and say a prayer for him"
But like Louise always says
"Ya can't look at much, can ya man?"
As she, herself, prepares for him
And Madonna, she still has not showed
We see this empty cage now corrode
Where her cape of the stage once had flowed
The fiddler, he now steps to the road
He writes ev'rything's been returned which was owed
On the back of the fish truck that loads
While my conscience explodes
The harmonicas play the skeleton keys and the rain
And these visions of Johanna are now all that remain

我们总有一个人要明白
（迟早的事）

不是故意对你那么坏
请不要觉得是针对你
不是故意要害你伤心
你只是刚好在那里，如此而已
看着你和朋友微笑说再见
我想一切都很明白
你应该很快会回来
却不知道那句再见，竟是诀别

只不过，迟早的事，我们总有一个人要明白
你只不过做了你该做的
迟早的事，我们总有一个人要明白
我真的曾经努力，想要靠紧你

我看不到你有什么，可以展露给我
围巾完全遮住了你的口
看不出你怎么可能了解我
但你说你了解，我就信了

你在耳畔悄悄问我
是要选你，还是选她一起远走
我不明白到底听到了什么
也不明白你还多么青春年少

只不过，迟早的事，我们总有一个人要明白
你只不过做了你该做的
迟早的事，我们总有一个人要明白
我真的曾经努力，想要靠紧你

我什么也看不见，雪开始下了
只能听见你的声音
看不出我俩何去何从
但你说你知道，我就信了
后来你又说，在我道歉的时候
你说之前只是要我，你并不真的出身农家
而我告诉你，在你挖我眼珠的时候
真的从不打算伤害你一分一毫

只不过，迟早的事，我们总有一个人要明白
你只不过做了你该做的
迟早的事，我们总有一个人要明白
我真的曾经努力，想要靠紧你

One of Us Must Know (Sooner or Later)

I didn't mean to treat you so bad
You shouldn't take it so personal
I didn't mean to make you so sad
You just happened to be there, that's all
When I saw you say "goodbye" to your friend and smile
I thought that it was well understood
That you'd be comin' back in a little while
I didn't know that you were sayin' "goodbye" for good

But, sooner or later, one of us must know
You just did what you're supposed to do
Sooner or later, one of us must know
That I really did try to get close to you

I couldn't see what you could show me
Your scarf had kept your mouth well hid
I couldn't see how you could know me
But you said you knew me and I believed you did
When you whispered in my ear
And asked me if I was leavin' with you or her
I didn't realize just what I did hear
I didn't realize how young you were

But, sooner or later, one of us must know
You just did what you're supposed to do
Sooner or later, one of us must know
That I really did try to get close to you

I couldn't see when it started snowin'
Your voice was all that I heard
I couldn't see where we were goin'
But you said you knew an' I took your word
And then you told me later, as I apologized
That you were just kiddin' me, you weren't really from the farm
An' I told you, as you clawed out my eyes
That I never really meant to do you any harm

But, sooner or later, one of us must know
You just did what you're supposed to do
Sooner or later, one of us must know
That I really did try to get close to you

我要你

认罪的殓尸人叹息
寂寞的手摇风琴师哭泣
银色萨克斯风说：我该拒绝你
裂开的铃，褪色的号角
吹向我的脸，尽情嘲笑
但是不该如此
我不该命中注定失去你

我要你，我要你
我好想好想要你
宝贝，我要你

烂醉的政客跳啊跳
跳到大街上，母亲都在哭泣
救主也都睡熟了，他们等着你
我等他们来叫停
叫我别从缺口的杯子痛饮
叫我打开大门
为了迎接你

我要你，我要你
我好想好想要你
宝贝，我要你

我的父辈，他们从来
竟不曾拥有真爱
但他们的女儿都瞧我不起
只因我从不在乎这些事情

呵，我回到黑桃皇后那边
和我那女仆聊聊天
她知道的，看着她我并不胆怯
她对我好
什么都瞒不过她的眼
她知道我喜欢去哪边
但一切都无所谓

我要你，我要你
我好想好想要你
宝贝，我要你

你那跳舞的孩子，一身中国衣裳
他找我说话，我抢走他的笛子

是啊，我不怎么讨他喜欢，对吧？

但我那么做，只因为他撒谎

因为他害你上当

因为时间站在他这边

因为我……

我要你，我要你

我好想好想要你

宝贝，我要你

I Want You

The guilty undertaker sighs
The lonesome organ grinder cries
The silver saxophones say I should refuse you
The cracked bells and washed-out horns
Blow into my face with scorn
But it's not that way
I wasn't born to lose you

I want you, I want you
I want you so bad
Honey, I want you

The drunken politician leaps
Upon the street where mothers weep
And the saviors who are fast asleep, they wait for you
And I wait for them to interrupt
Me drinkin' from my broken cup
And ask me to
Open up the gate for you

I want you, I want you
I want you so bad
Honey, I want you

How all my fathers, they've gone down
True love they've been without it
But all their daughters put me down
'Cause I don't think about it

Well, I return to the Queen of Spades
And talk with my chambermaid
She knows that I'm not afraid to look at her
She is good to me
And there's nothing she doesn't see
She knows where I'd like to be
But it doesn't matter

I want you, I want you
I want you so bad
Honey, I want you

Now your dancing child with his Chinese suit
He spoke to me, I took his flute
No, I wasn't very cute to him, was I?
But I did it, though, because he lied
Because he took you for a ride
And because time was on his side
And because I…

I want you, I want you
I want you so bad
Honey, I want you

再次困在莫比尔和孟菲斯蓝调一起[1]

噢，收破烂的在地上画着圈
走来走去踏着同一条街
我想问问他出了什么事
可我知道他不说话
女士对我都很好
拿胶带替我装点
我心底其实明白
怎么也逃不出去
唉，妈妈啊，能不能终于有个了局
再次困在莫比尔
和孟菲斯蓝调一起

莎士比亚，他在小巷
穿尖头鞋戴铃铛
和法国姑娘聊天
她说跟我很熟

1. 莫比尔，位于美国亚拉巴马州。亚拉巴马州为乡村、蓝调音乐重镇，被誉为“蓝调之父”的汉迪（W. C. Handy）即生于此。孟菲斯蓝调，指涉汉迪的同名歌曲，乃“蓝调”一词最早的书面记录。

我本会捎个信
看看她到底曾否开口
可是整间邮局都被偷走
连信箱也上锁
唉，妈妈啊，能不能终于有个了局
再次困在莫比尔
和孟菲斯蓝调一起

莫娜想要警告我
千万远离火车路线
她说那些铁道员
喝酒一样喝干你的血
我说：“喔，没听过这种事
话说回来，以前也只遇见一个
那人朝我眼皮喷一口烟
又一拳揍上我叼的香烟”
唉，妈妈啊，能不能终于有个了局
再次困在莫比尔
和孟菲斯蓝调一起

爷爷上星期死了
已经埋在石堆的坟冢
但人人都还在议论

事发当时多么惊恐
我呢，却早有预感
我知道他已经失控
竟在大街生起火
又轰得它满是弹孔
唉，妈妈啊，能不能终于有个了局
再次困在莫比尔
和孟菲斯蓝调一起

参议员也到场
对每个人亮枪
又赠票给大家
来吃他儿子的喜酒
我呢，却差点被逮去坐牢
该要算我好运气
万一被发现逃票
还被抓到躲在卡车底
唉，妈妈啊，能不能终于有个了局
再次困在莫比尔
和孟菲斯蓝调一起

牧师觉得我不可理喻
竟然问他为何打扮起来

二十磅重的新闻头条
通通钉在胸口招摇
我指给他看，却被辱骂诅咒
只好偷偷对他说："连你也躲不过
你看，你就像我
但愿你称心满意"
唉，妈妈啊，能不能终于有个了局
再次困在莫比尔
和孟菲斯蓝调一起

雨人给我灵药两帖
然后说："上来试试看"
一帖是得州神药[1]
一帖是铁道杜松子酒
我真蠢，把两帖混在一块
果然害我神魂颠倒
如今人人嘴脸丑陋
时间感也不存在
唉，妈妈啊，能不能终于有个了局
再次困在莫比尔

1. 得州神药，致幻剂麦司卡林（Mescaline）俗称，以美墨边境生长的仙人掌提炼而成。

和孟菲斯蓝调一起

露丝要我来看她
在她酒吧音乐的潟湖
看她跳华尔兹，钱不用付
映着她那巴拿马的月光
我说：“少来啦
你一定知道我那初见世面的新人”
她说：“那个新人只懂你的需要
我却看穿你的渴望”
唉，妈妈啊，能不能终于有个了局
再次困在莫比尔
和孟菲斯蓝调一起

地砖铺在格兰街
霓虹疯人往上攀
然后跌回街上，完美圆满
时机更是分毫不差
我坐在这儿耐心守候
想知道要付出多少代价
才能摆脱这一切
不必从头再来一回
唉，妈妈啊，能不能终于有个了局

再次困在莫比尔

和孟菲斯蓝调一起

Stuck Inside of Mobile with the Memphis Blues Again

Oh, the ragman draws circles
Up and down the block
I'd ask him what the matter was
But I know that he don't talk
And the ladies treat me kindly
And furnish me with tape
But deep inside my heart
I know I can't escape
Oh, Mama, can this really be the end
To be stuck inside of Mobile
With the Memphis blues again

Well, Shakespeare, he's in the alley
With his pointed shoes and his bells
Speaking to some French girl
Who says she knows me well
And I would send a message
To find out if she's talked
But the post office has been stolen
And the mailbox is locked
Oh, Mama, can this really be the end
To be stuck inside of Mobile
With the Memphis blues again

Mona tried to tell me
To stay away from the train line
She said that all the railroad men
Just drink up your blood like wine

An' I said, "Oh, I didn't know that
But then again, there's only one I've met
An' he just smoked my eyelids
An' punched my cigarette"
Oh, Mama, can this really be the end
To be stuck inside of Mobile
With the Memphis blues again

Grandpa died last week
And now he's buried in the rocks
But everybody still talks about
How badly they were shocked
But me, I expected it to happen
I knew he'd lost control
When he built a fire on Main Street
And shot it full of holes
Oh, Mama, can this really be the end
To be stuck inside of Mobile
With the Memphis blues again

Now the senator came down here
Showing ev'ryone his gun
Handing out free tickets
To the wedding of his son
An' me, I nearly got busted
An' wouldn't it be my luck
To get caught without a ticket
And be discovered beneath a truck
Oh, Mama, can this really be the end
To be stuck inside of Mobile
With the Memphis blues again

Now the preacher looked so baffled

When I asked him why he dressed
With twenty pounds of headlines
Stapled to his chest
But he cursed me when I proved it to him
Then I whispered, "Not even you can hide
You see, you're just like me
I hope you're satisfied"
Oh, Mama, can this really be the end
To be stuck inside of Mobile
With the Memphis blues again

Now the rainman gave me two cures
Then he said, "Jump right in"
The one was Texas medicine
The other was just railroad gin
An' like a fool I mixed them
An' it strangled up my mind
An' now people just get uglier
An' I have no sense of time
Oh, Mama, can this really be the end
To be stuck inside of Mobile
With the Memphis blues again

When Ruthie says come see her
In her honky-tonk lagoon
Where I can watch her waltz for free
'Neath her Panamanian moon
An' I say, "Aw come on now
You must know about my debutante"
An' she says, "Your debutante just knows what you need
But I know what you want"
Oh, Mama, can this really be the end
To be stuck inside of Mobile

With the Memphis blues again

Now the bricks lay on Grand Street
Where the neon madmen climb
They all fall there so perfectly
It all seems so well timed
An' here I sit so patiently
Waiting to find out what price
You have to pay to get out of
Going through all these things twice
Oh, Mama, can this really be the end
To be stuck inside of Mobile
With the Memphis blues again

豹纹图样药盒形状的帽子[1]

有的，看到你戴上了那顶全新的豹纹图样药盒形状的帽子
对的，看到你戴上了那顶全新的豹纹图样药盒形状的帽子
嘿，一定要告诉我，宝贝
你的脑袋放在那玩意底下是什么滋味
一顶全新的豹纹图样药盒形状的帽子

嘿，你戴着它很漂亮
宝贝，我可不可以偶尔在上面跳一跳？
对，我只想知道
它是不是那种特别名贵的式样？
知道吧？它不偏不倚摆在你头顶
就像一张床垫
不偏不倚顶在一只酒瓶
你那顶全新的豹纹图样药盒形状的帽子

嘿，要是你想看日出

1. 原为加拿大西北骑警的军帽，经美国设计师罗伊·弗罗威克（Roy Halston Frowick）之手后，成为时尚潮流。杰奎琳·肯尼迪在丈夫总统就职演说时戴的就是这种帽子。

宝贝，我知道该去哪
嘿，我们哪天一起去看日出吧
我们俩就坐着傻看
我会有一条皮带
绑着脑袋
你呢也坐在那儿
戴着你那顶全新的豹纹图样药盒形状的帽子

嘿，我问医生能不能来找你
那样有碍健康，他说
对啦，我违反他的禁令
跑来看你
结果发现他在你这里
知道吗？我不介意他把我当冤大头
可我真想叫他把那玩意从头上摘走
你那顶全新的豹纹图样药盒形状的帽子

嘿，看到你有新男友
知道吗，我以前没见过那个人
嘿，我看到他
和你做爱
你俩忘了关上车库门
也许你以为他爱你是为了你的钱

我却知道他爱上你真正的原因
你那顶全新的豹纹图样药盒形状的帽子

Leopard-Skin Pill-Box Hat

Well, I see you got your brand new leopard-skin pill-box hat
Yes, I see you got your brand new leopard-skin pill-box hat
Well, you must tell me, baby
How your head feels under somethin' like that
Under your brand new leopard-skin pill-box hat

Well, you look so pretty in it
Honey, can I jump on it sometime?
Yes, I just wanna see
If it's really that expensive kind
You know it balances on your head
Just like a mattress balances
On a bottle of wine
Your brand new leopard-skin pill-box hat

Well, if you wanna see the sun rise
Honey, I know where
We'll go out and see it sometime
We'll both just sit there and stare
Me with my belt
Wrapped around my head
And you just sittin' there
In your brand new leopard-skin pill-box hat

Well, I asked the doctor if I could see you
It's bad for your health, he said
Yes, I disobeyed his orders
I came to see you
But I found him there instead

You know, I don't mind him cheatin' on me
But I sure wish he'd take that off his head
Your brand new leopard-skin pill-box hat

Well, I see you got a new boyfriend
You know, I never seen him before
Well, I saw him
Makin' love to you
You forgot to close the garage door
You might think he loves you for your money
But I know what he really loves you for
It's your brand new leopard-skin pill-box hat

就像个女人

没有谁感到丝毫痛苦
今夜，我就站在雨里
谁都知道
宝贝有了新衣裳
但不久前我才见到，她的缎带和蝴蝶结
从她的卷发垂落
她要了，就像个女人，是啊
她做爱，就像个女人，是啊
她疼痛，就像个女人
然而她破碎，像个小女孩

玛丽女皇，她是我的朋友
是啊，我们应该还会相见
没有谁会怀疑
宝贝不会得到祝福
除非终于认清，她和所有人都一样
包括她的雾，她的安非他命，还有她的珍珠
她要了，就像个女人，是啊
她做爱，就像个女人，是啊
她疼痛，就像个女人

然而她破碎，像个小女孩

是啊，雨一开始就不曾停止
我却在那儿几乎渴死
所以我走进此处
而你久远的咒诅仍然狠毒
更糟糕的是
这里的痛苦
我无法留在此处
难道一切还不够清楚？

我就是无法融入
是啊，时候到了，应该做个结束
但当我俩重逢
当成普通朋友引介彼此
请千万不要透露，你曾与我相识
那时我饥饿不已，世界却属于你
啊，你伪装，就像个女人，是啊
你做爱，就像个女人，是啊
然后你疼痛，就像个女人
但你破碎，像个小女孩

Just Like a Woman

Nobody feels any pain
Tonight as I stand inside the rain
Ev'rybody knows
That Baby's got new clothes
But lately I see her ribbons and her bows
Have fallen from her curls
She takes just like a woman, yes, she does
She makes love just like a woman, yes, she does
And she aches just like a woman
But she breaks just like a little girl

Queen Mary, she's my friend
Yes, I believe I'll go see her again
Nobody has to guess
That Baby can't be blessed
Till she sees finally that she's like all the rest
With her fog, her amphetamine and her pearls
She takes just like a woman, yes, she does
She makes love just like a woman, yes, she does
And she aches just like a woman
But she breaks just like a little girl

It was raining from the first
And I was dying there of thirst
So I came in here
And your long-time curse hurts
But what's worse
Is this pain in here
I can't stay in here

Ain't it clear that—

I just can't fit
Yes, I believe it's time for us to quit
When we meet again
Introduced as friends
Please don't let on that you knew me when
I was hungry and it was your world
Ah, you fake just like a woman, yes, you do
You make love just like a woman, yes, you do
Then you ache just like a woman
But you break just like a little girl

多半是你走你的路
（我过我的桥）

你说你爱我
还说你想着我
知道吗，你或许会搞错
你说你告诉过我
说想要抱住我
知道吗，你没那么强壮
我就是没办法重来一次
也没办法继续哀求
我打算让你先走
而我殿后
时间会证明一切，到底谁跌跤
又是谁被甩在后头
且让你走你的路，我过我的桥

你说你扰乱了我
还说你配不上我
知道吗，你有时候会胡说
你说你全身颤抖

始终感觉好痛
可你心里知道，自己付出多少
有时候已经没办法在乎
事情总不能永远像这样
我打算让你先走
是啊，而我殿后
时间会证明一切，到底谁跌跤
又是谁被甩在后头
且让你走你的路，我过我的桥

法官心存恨意
他会来拜访你
不过他体格欠佳
还踩着一副高跷
小心，别让他跌到你身上

你说很对不起
之前编了故事
你知道我深信不疑
你说你找到个
不一样的情人
很好，我不怀疑
你说我的吻和他不相似

可是这一次，我再也不要向你解释

我打算让你先走

是啊，而我殿后

时间会证明一切，到底谁跌跤

又是谁被甩在后头

且让你走你的路，我过我的桥

Most Likely You Go Your Way (and I'll Go Mine)

You say you love me
And you're thinkin' of me
But you know you could be wrong
You say you told me
That you wanna hold me
But you know you're not that strong
I just can't do what I done before
I just can't beg you anymore
I'm gonna let you pass
And I'll go last
Then time will tell just who fell
And who's been left behind
When you go your way and I go mine

You say you disturb me
And you don't deserve me
But you know sometimes you lie
You say you're shakin'
And you're always achin'
But you know how hard you try
Sometimes it gets so hard to care
It can't be this way ev'rywhere
And I'm gonna let you pass
Yes, and I'll go last
Then time will tell just who fell
And who's been left behind
When you go your way and I go mine

The judge, he holds a grudge
He's gonna call on you
But he's badly built
And he walks on stilts
Watch out he don't fall on you

You say you're sorry
For tellin' stories
That you know I believe are true
You say ya got some
Other kinda lover
And yes, I believe you do
You say my kisses are not like his
But this time I'm not gonna tell you why that is
I'm just gonna let you pass
Yes, and I'll go last
Then time will tell who fell
And who's been left behind
When you go your way and I go mine

一时就像阿喀琉斯

站在你窗前，宝贝
是啊，我以前就来过
我是如此温驯无害
望着你那二道门
为何对我不闻不问？
明明知道我要你的爱
宝贝，为何如此铁石心肠？

在你屋里跪下
是啊，我还是流连不走
想要审视你的画像，但是
我好无助，简直像个富二代
为什么派人把我挡在门外？
明明知道我要你的爱
宝贝，为何如此铁石心肠？

简直像个蠢蛋，风华正盛
是啊我知道，你听得到我的脚步声
就不知道你的心，是石头造的，是石灰做的
还是岩块凿的？

冲进你的门厅

靠着你的丝绒大门

眼看你的蝎子

爬过你的马戏场

到底你有什么，必须死守不放？

明明知道我要你的爱

宝贝，但是你如此铁石心肠

阿喀琉斯站在你的小巷

他不让我留下，他满口大话

手指朝天举起

十分饥渴，像汉子扮了女装

你怎么了，身边的卫士竟是这样？

明明知道我要你的爱

宝贝，但是你如此铁石心肠

Temporary Like Achilles

Standing on your window, honey
Yes, I've been here before
Feeling so harmless
I'm looking at your second door
How come you don't send me no regards?
You know I want your lovin'
Honey, why are you so hard?

Kneeling 'neath your ceiling
Yes, I guess I'll be here for a while
I'm tryin' to read your portrait, but
I'm helpless, like a rich man's child
How come you send someone out to have me barred?
You know I want your lovin'
Honey, why are you so hard?

Like a poor fool in his prime
Yes, I know you can hear me walk
But is your heart made out of stone, or is it lime
Or is it just solid rock?

Well, I rush into your hallway
Lean against your velvet door
I watch upon your scorpion
Who crawls across your circus floor
Just what do you think you have to guard?
You know I want your lovin'
Honey, but you're so hard

Achilles is in your alleyway
He don't want me here, he does brag
He's pointing to the sky
And he's hungry, like a man in drag
How come you get someone like him to be your guard?
You know I want your lovin'
Honey, but you're so hard

绝对甜蜜的玛丽

嘿，你的平交道，我没法跳
有时很不容易，你知道
我只能坐着，敲敲小号
回想每个你许下的诺言
但是今晚你在哪里，甜蜜玛丽？

嘿，我等过你，带着半病的身体
嗯，我等过你，在你恨我的时期
嘿，我等过你，在纹风不动的车阵里
而你明明知道，我得赶去别地
但是今晚你在哪里，甜蜜玛丽？

嘿，每个人都能跟我一样，这是明白的道理
不过话说回来，没几个人学得了你，也算好运气

六匹白马，你曾应许
终于送去了监狱
但要做法外之徒，你总得诚实面对自己
我记得，你总是说你也同意
但是今晚你在哪里，甜蜜玛丽？

嘿，怎么回事我也弄不清
但是河船的老大，他知道我的命
然而其他所有人，包括你
都得继续等到底

嘿，一场高烧在我口袋里
喝醉的波斯人，跟着我一起
我愿带他去你家，但是开不了锁
可知道，你忘了把钥匙留给我
喔，今晚你在哪里，甜蜜玛丽？

喏，坐牢的时候，每封信都提醒我
谁都不该把地址泄漏给帮众团伙
如今我看着你泛黄的铁路，站在这里
在你阳台的遗迹
想着今晚你在哪里，甜蜜玛丽

Absolutely Sweet Marie

Well, your railroad gate, you know I just can't jump it
Sometimes it gets so hard, you see
I'm just sitting here beating on my trumpet
With all these promises you left for me
But where are you tonight, sweet Marie?

Well, I waited for you when I was half sick
Yes, I waited for you when you hated me
Well, I waited for you inside of the frozen traffic
When you knew I had some other place to be
Now, where are you tonight, sweet Marie?

Well, anybody can be just like me, obviously
But then, now again, not too many can be like you, fortunately

Well, six white horses that you did promise
Were fin'lly delivered down to the penitentiary
But to live outside the law, you must be honest
I know you always say that you agree
But where are you tonight, sweet Marie?

Well, I don't know how it happened
But the riverboat captain, he knows my fate
But ev'rybody else, even yourself
They're just gonna have to wait

Well, I got the fever down in my pockets
The Persian drunkard, he follows me
Yes, I can take him to your house but I can't unlock it

You see, you forgot to leave me with the key
Oh, where are you tonight, sweet Marie?

Now, I been in jail when all my mail showed
That a man can't give his address out to bad company
And now I stand here lookin' at your yellow railroad
In the ruins of your balcony
Wond'ring where you are tonight, sweet Marie

第四次左右

她说
“省省吧，都是谎话”
我大喊说她聋啦
她对付我的脸，直到眼眶裂开
又说：“你还有什么剩下？”
是了，就在那一刻，我起身离开
但她又说：“记好了
谁都必须为到手的东西
付出代价”

我站在那里，哼着歌
轻轻敲着她的鼓，问她：“怎么啦？”
她扣好靴子
理好衣装
然后说：“不必假模假样”
我只好勉强摸进口袋
拇指翻翻找找
殷勤地拿给她
我仅剩的最后一片口香糖

她把我撵了出来
我站在尘土里，人们摩肩擦踵
发现忘了拿上衣
我回去敲门
在门厅等她进屋去拿
努力想搞清楚
那幅画面：你坐着轮椅
轮椅靠着……

她的牙买加朗姆酒
她总算来了，我也要一点尝尝
她说："不给，亲爱的"
我说："你口齿不清
要不要先吐掉口香糖"
她连声尖叫，满脸通红
然后倒地不起
我把她盖好，想了想
应该翻翻她的抽屉

当我做好处理
就都放进鞋里
带来给你
你呢，带我进来这里

就这样爱上我

半点时间也不浪费

我呢，我从来都不贪心

我永远不会要你那副拐杖

所以，也请别打我那副的主意

Fourth Time Around

When she said
"Don't waste your words, they're just lies"
I cried she was deaf
And she worked on my face until breaking my eyes
Then said, "What else you got left?"
It was then that I got up to leave
But she said, "Don't forget
Everybody must give something back
For something they get"

I stood there and hummed
I tapped on her drum and asked her how come
And she buttoned her boot
And straightened her suit
Then she said, "Don't get cute"
So I forced my hands in my pockets
And felt with my thumbs
And gallantly handed her
My very last piece of gum

She threw me outside
I stood in the dirt where ev'ryone walked
And after finding I'd
Forgotten my shirt
I went back and knocked
I waited in the hallway, she went to get it
And I tried to make sense
Out of that picture of you in your wheelchair
That leaned up against...

Her Jamaican rum
And when she did come, I asked her for some
She said, "No, dear"
I said, "Your words aren't clear
You'd better spit out your gum"
She screamed till her face got so red
Then she fell on the floor
And I covered her up and then
Thought I'd go look through her drawer

And when I was through
I filled up my shoe
And brought it to you
And you, you took me in
You loved me then
You didn't waste time
And I, I never took much
I never asked for your crutch
Now don't ask for mine

分明五位信徒

一大清早
一大清早
我呼唤你
我呼唤你
快回家
没有你，我或许还是可以
只要不再感觉这么孤寂

别害我失望
别害我失望
我不会让你失望
我不会让你失望
我不会
知道吗，你可以我也可以，宝贝
但是宝贝，拜托别这样

我那条黑狗在叫
黑狗在叫
是啊它在叫
是啊它在叫

在我院子外面
是啊，我想告诉你它的意见
只要我之前不必那么拼

你妈在干活
你妈在哀哀叫
她在哭啊，知道吧
她在拼命，知道吧
你还是赶快走啦
嘿，我很想告诉你她要的是啥
可是不知如何开口啊

十五个杂耍艺人[1]
十五个杂耍艺人
五个信徒
五个信徒
都扮成男人样
告诉你妈别担心，因为
大家都是我的朋友

一大清早

---

1. 杂耍艺人，亦有"骗子""毒贩"之意。

一大清早

我呼唤你

我呼唤你

快回家

没有你，我或许还是可以

只要不再感觉这么孤寂

Obviously Five Believers

Early in the mornin'
Early in the mornin'
I'm callin' you to
I'm callin' you to
Please come home
Yes, I guess I could make it without you
If I just didn't feel so all alone

Don't let me down
Don't let me down
I won't let you down
I won't let you down
No I won't
You know I can if you can, honey
But, honey, please don't

I got my black dog barkin'
Black dog barkin'
Yes it is now
Yes it is now
Outside my yard
Yes, I could tell you what he means
If I just didn't have to try so hard

Your mama's workin'
Your mama's moanin'
She's cryin' you know
She's tryin' you know
You better go now

Well, I'd tell you what she wants
But I just don't know how

Fifteen jugglers
Fifteen jugglers
Five believers
Five believers
All dressed like men
Tell yo' mama not to worry because
They're just my friends

Early in the mornin'
Early in the mornin'
I'm callin' you to
I'm callin' you to
Please come home
Yes, I could make it without you
If I just did not feel so all alone

满眼忧伤的低地女士[1]

凭你水银的嘴，在传教士的时代
你烟样的眼，和诗韵似的祷词
你银铸的十字，和钟鸣似的嗓子
噢，他们有谁，竟以为能葬了你？
凭你的口袋，如今妥善收起
你街车的幻景，投在青草地
你的肉体似绢丝，面容似玻璃
他们有谁，竟以为能背负你？
满眼忧伤的低地女士
在彼处，满眼忧伤的先知说：并无男人到此
我仓库的眼，我的阿拉伯鼓
是否都该留在你门口？
还是，满眼忧伤的女士，我该继续守候？

凭你银光闪闪的床单，你蕾丝般的腰带
你的那副扑克牌，缺失了 J 和 A
你地窖的衣裳，你空洞的脸庞

---

1. 这首歌写给第一任妻子萨拉·朗兹（Sara Lownds），迪伦将她的姓名织入歌名。

他们有谁，竟以为能看穿你？
凭你的侧影，暮色映入双眼
月光泅泳其间
你火柴的歌，和吉普赛圣诗
他们有谁，竟企图要打动你？
满眼忧伤的低地女士
在彼处，满眼忧伤的先知说：并无男人到此
我仓库的眼，我的阿拉伯鼓
是否都该留在你门口？
还是，满眼忧伤的女士，我该继续守候？

推罗的列王带着罪人的清单
排队等待天竺葵那一吻
你不明白何以如此
可是他们有谁，真心只想吻你？
凭你儿时的火焰，烧着夜半的毛毯
你西班牙的仪态，和母亲的药
你牛仔的口，和宵禁的栓
他们有谁，你以为，可能抗拒你？
满眼忧伤的低地女士
在彼处，满眼忧伤的先知说：并无男人到此
我仓库的眼，我的阿拉伯鼓
是否都该留在你门口？

还是，满眼忧伤的女士，我该继续守候？

噢，农民和商人，他们都做好决定
让你看天使的尸体，之前只敢偷偷藏起
但为何他们选了你，以为这边你会同情？
噢，怎么会这样误会你？
他们愿你揽下农家的过失
但是凭你脚下的大海，你虚张声势的警报
凭那恶棍的小孩，你紧抱在臂怀
他们怎么可能，怎么可能劝服你？
满眼忧伤的低地女士
在彼处，满眼忧伤的先知说：并无男人到此
我仓库的眼，我的阿拉伯鼓
是否都该留在你门口？
还是，满眼忧伤的女士，我该继续守候？

凭你在罐头厂街，那铁片的记忆
你的杂志丈夫，总有一天要分离
你的温柔，如今再也藏不起
他们有谁，你以为会聘了你？
如今你傍着你的贼，你在他的假释期
凭你神圣的奖章，指尖就能折起
你圣人样的面容，你鬼魅般的灵魂

噢，他们有谁，你以为可能毁灭你？
满眼忧伤的低地女士
在彼处，满眼忧伤的先知说：并无男人到此
我仓库的眼，我的阿拉伯鼓
是否都该留在你门口？
还是，满眼忧伤的女士，我该继续守候？

Sad-Eyed Lady of the Lowlands

With your mercury mouth in the missionary times
And your eyes like smoke and your prayers like rhymes
And your silver cross, and your voice like chimes
Oh, who among them do they think could bury you?
With your pockets well protected at last
And your streetcar visions which you place on the grass
And your flesh like silk, and your face like glass
Who among them do they think could carry you?
Sad-eyed lady of the lowlands
Where the sad-eyed prophet says that no man comes
My warehouse eyes, my Arabian drums
Should I leave them by your gate
Or, sad-eyed lady, should I wait?

With your sheets like metal and your belt like lace
And your deck of cards missing the jack and the ace
And your basement clothes and your hollow face
Who among them can think he could outguess you?
With your silhouette when the sunlight dims
Into your eyes where the moonlight swims
And your matchbook songs and your gypsy hymns
Who among them would try to impress you?
Sad-eyed lady of the lowlands
Where the sad-eyed prophet says that no man comes
My warehouse eyes, my Arabian drums
Should I leave them by your gate
Or, sad-eyed lady, should I wait?

The kings of Tyrus with their convict list

Are waiting in line for their geranium kiss
And you wouldn't know it would happen like this
But who among them really wants just to kiss you?
With your childhood flames on your midnight rug
And your Spanish manners and your mother's drugs
And your cowboy mouth and your curfew plugs
Who among them do you think could resist you?
Sad-eyed lady of the lowlands
Where the sad-eyed prophet says that no man comes
My warehouse eyes, my Arabian drums
Should I leave them by your gate
Or, sad-eyed lady, should I wait?

Oh, the farmers and the businessmen, they all did decide
To show you the dead angels that they used to hide
But why did they pick you to sympathize with their side?
Oh, how could they ever mistake you?
They wished you'd accepted the blame for the farm
But with the sea at your feet and the phony false alarm
And with the child of a hoodlum wrapped up in your arms
How could they ever, ever persuade you?
Sad-eyed lady of the lowlands
Where the sad-eyed prophet says that no man comes
My warehouse eyes, my Arabian drums
Should I leave them by your gate
Or, sad-eyed lady, should I wait?

With your sheet-metal memory of Cannery Row
And your magazine-husband who one day just had to go
And your gentleness now, which you just can't help but show
Who among them do you think would employ you?
Now you stand with your thief, you're on his parole

With your holy medallion which your fingertips fold
And your saintlike face and your ghostlike soul
Oh, who among them do you think could destroy you?
Sad-eyed lady of the lowlands
Where the sad-eyed prophet says that no man comes
My warehouse eyes, my Arabian drums
Should I leave them by your gate
Or, sad-eyed lady, should I wait?

我会把它当自己的事

你要去寻找，宝贝
不惜代价
但是要找多久，宝贝
找你并没丢失的东西？
大家都会帮你
一些人很有善意
但是如果我能帮你节省些时间
来吧，这事儿交给我
我会把它当自己的事

我忍不住
即便你可能把我当怪物
即便我说我爱你不是因为你是什么
而是因为你不是什么
大家都会帮你
找到你一直在找的东西
但是如果我能帮你节省些时间
来吧，这事儿交给我
我会把它当自己的事

火车离开

在十点半

但是明天同一时间

它还会再回来

售票员疲惫不堪

他仍然困在这条线上

但是如果我能帮你节省些时间

来吧，这事儿交给我

我会把它当自己的事

I'll Keep It with Mine

You will search, babe
At any cost
But how long, babe
Can you search for what's not lost?
Everybody will help you
Some people are very kind
But if I can save you any time
Come on, give it to me
I'll keep it with mine

I can't help it
If you might think I'm odd
If I say I'm not loving you for what you are
But for what you're not
Everybody will help you
Discover what you set out to find
But if I can save you any time
Come on, give it to me
I'll keep it with mine

The train leaves
At half past ten
But it'll be back tomorrow
Same time again
The conductor he's weary
He's still stuck on the line
But if I can save you any time
Come on, give it to me
I'll keep it with mine

我要做你情人

哦，雨人带着他的魔杖来了
而法官说："莫娜不能被保释"
墙相撞，莫娜大哭
雨人披着狼人的伪装离去

我要做你情人，宝贝，我要做你男人
我要做你情人，宝贝
不做她的情人，要做你的

哦，入殓师穿着午夜礼服
对蒙面人说："你好帅！"
哦，蒙面人从高阁上起了身
说："你也不赖"

我要做你情人，宝贝，我要做你男人
我要做你情人，宝贝
不做她的情人，要做你的

哦，“跳跳朱迪”[1]再不能跳更高
她的眼里有子弹，它们开着火
拉斯普京[2]仪态如此庄重
他摸到她的后脑，然后他死了

我要做你情人，宝贝，我要做你男人
我要做你情人，宝贝
不做她的情人，要做你的

哦，淮德拉[3]带着明镜
身体舒展地躺在那草坪
她把一切都弄乱了套，她晕了
那是因为她外露，而你不同

我要做你情人，宝贝，我要做你男人
我要做你情人，宝贝
不做她的情人，要做你的

1.“跳跳朱迪”，美国囚歌中的女性形象，一般认为名字含遭受鞭笞而跳起之意。

2. 拉斯普京（Grigori Rasputin，1869—1916），俄国神秘主义者，沙皇尼古拉二世的宠臣。

3. 淮德拉，希腊神话中雅典国王忒修斯的后妻，钟情国王前妻之子希波吕托斯，因求爱不遂，羞怒诬蔑希波吕托斯强奸了自己。

I Wanna Be Your Lover

Well, the rainman comes with his magic wand
And the judge says, "Mona can't have no bond"
And the walls collide, Mona cries
And the rainman leaves in the wolfman's disguise

I wanna be your lover, baby, I wanna be your man
I wanna be your lover, baby
I don't wanna be hers, I wanna be yours

Well, the undertaker in his midnight suit
Says to the masked man, "Ain't you cute!"
Well, the mask man he gets up on the shelf
And he says, "You ain't so bad yourself"

I wanna be your lover, baby, I wanna be your man
I wanna be your lover, baby
I don't wanna be hers, I wanna be yours

Well, jumpin' Judy can't go no higher
She had bullets in her eyes, and they fire
Rasputin he's so dignified
He touched the back of her head an' he died

I wanna be your lover, baby, I wanna be your man
I wanna be your lover, baby
I don't wanna be hers, I wanna be yours

Well, Phaedra with her looking glass
Stretchin' out upon the grass

She gets all messed up and she faints—
That's 'cause she's so obvious and you ain't

I wanna be your lover, baby, I wanna be your man
I wanna be your lover, baby
I don't wanna be hers, I wanna be yours

告诉我，妈妈

老黑巴斯康[1]，别打了镜子
冷黑水犬，千万莫流泪
你说你爱我，说那可能是爱情
你记不起来你示过爱了宝贝？
弄好了蒸汽钻，你去找男孩儿
让它为你干活儿，好像你的九磅铁锤[2]
但是我知道你知道我知道你的表情说明
有什么正在撕裂你的心

告诉我，妈妈
告诉我，妈妈
告诉我，妈妈，发生了什么？
这回你是怎么啦？

---

1. 指巴斯康·伦斯福德（Bascom Lamar Lunsford，1882—1973），美国民俗音乐学家，致力搜集传统民谣。
2. 以上两行歌词指涉19世纪美国民间故事，传说在开凿切萨皮克与俄亥俄铁路的大本德隧道时，黑人钢钻工约翰·亨利与蒸汽钻比赛在岩石上打炮眼，虽然最后亨利获胜，但劳累致死。许多劳动号子、民谣以此题材为曲，如《九磅铁锤》。

喂，约翰，来时给我带些甜品
唉，这感觉真像是身陷于密林
在一月旅行上花费些时日
你找到墓碑驼鹿耸起和你的墓地鞭子
若你急于知道友情何时到头
来吧宝贝，我是你的朋友！
而我知道你知道我知道你的表情说明
有什么正在撕裂你的心

告诉我，妈妈
告诉我，妈妈
告诉我，妈妈，发生了什么？
这回你是怎么啦？

哦，操这编辑，我们实在读不懂
但他的彩绘雪橇，其实是张床
是的，我看见你在窗台上
但是我说不清你离那边缘有多远
而不管怎么说，你只是想要人跳和喊
你要去干那事是为了什么？
因为我知道你知道我知道你知道
有什么正在撕裂你的心

啊，告诉我，妈妈

告诉我，妈妈

告诉我，妈妈，发生了什么?

这回你是怎么啦?

Tell Me, Momma

Ol' black Bascom, don't break no mirrors
Cold black water dog, make no tears
You say you love me with what may be love
Don't you remember makin' baby love?
Got your steam drill built and you're lookin' for some kid
To get it to work for you like your nine-pound hammer did
But I know that you know that I know that you show
Something is tearing up your mind

Tell me, momma
Tell me, momma
Tell me, momma, what is it?
What's wrong with you this time?

Hey, John, come and get me some candy goods
Shucks, it sure feels like it's in the woods
Spend some time on your January trips
You got tombstone moose up and your grave-yard whips
If you're anxious to find out when your friendship's gonna end
Come on, baby, I'm your friend!
And I know that you know that I know that you show
Something is tearing up your mind

Tell me, momma
Tell me, momma
Tell me, momma, what is it?
What's wrong with you this time?

Ohh, we bone the editor, can't get read
But his painted sled, instead it's a bed
Yes, I see you on your window ledge
But I can't tell just how far away you are from the edge
And, anyway, you're just gonna make people jump and roar
Watcha wanna go and do that for?
For I know that you know that I know that you know
Something is tearing up your mind

Ah, tell me, momma
Tell me, momma
Tell me, momma, what is it?
What's wrong with you this time?

她现在是你的人了

当铺老板狂笑
房东也、也、也在叫
场面太疯狂了，不是吗？
他们二位是如此开心
看到我毁掉了我从前的一切
痛苦确实能发掘出人最好的一面，不是吗？
假如你不想待，为何你不干脆离开？
为何非要对我这么坏？
非得这样吗？
这会儿你站在这，希望我记起你忘记说的事
是的，而你，我看见你仍和她在一起，呃
好吧因为她正在变得这么奇怪，你看不出来？
最好有人解释
她有她的铁索
这事儿我会做，但是我，不记得怎么做了
你去对她说吧
她现在是你的人了

我假想过
我们是在重罪室里

但我不是法官，你没必要讨好我
但请你把那情况
告诉你戴牛仔帽的朋友
你知道他一直对我把话说两遍
你知道我对你很坦率
你知道我从没打算要你做任何改变
你知道假如你不想和我在一块儿
你就可以……没必要待
现在你站这儿说你已原谅并忘记。亲爱的，我能说什么？
是的，你，你只是坐那儿说要烟灰缸，你够不着吗？
我见你吻她的脸，每次当她大谈起
她的金字塔画册
和比利小子[1]的明信片（凭什么每个人都得鞠躬？）
你最好跟她谈谈这些
现在你是她的人了

哦，在乎这事的每一位
都将爬上那城堡的楼梯
但是我不在你的城堡里，亲爱的
的的确确，圣弗兰西斯科我完全
想不起来了

---

1. 比利小子（Billy the Kid，1859—1881），美国西部著名枪手。

我甚至记不起埃尔帕索，哦亲爱的

你用不着非得忠诚

我不想要你悲痛

啊，这事为何对你来说这么难

假如你不想和我待，那就离开啊？

这会儿你站在这，手指伸进了我的袖子

那么你，究竟要做什么？你不是已经无话可说？

过不一会儿她就要站到吧台上

手里拿着鱼头和鱼叉

眉毛上粘着假胡子

你最好赶紧去做点儿什么

她现在是你的人了

She's Your Lover Now

The pawnbroker roared
Also, so, so did the landlord
The scene was so crazy, wasn't it?
Both were so glad
To watch me destroy what I had
Pain sure brings out the best in people, doesn't it?
Why didn't you just leave me if you didn't want to stay?
Why'd you have to treat me so bad?
Did it have to be that way?
Now you stand here expectin' me to remember somethin'
you forgot to say
Yes, and you, I see you're still with her, well
That's fine 'cause she's comin' on so strange, can't you tell?
Somebody had better explain
She's got her iron chain
I'd do it, but I, I just can't remember how
You talk to her
She's your lover now

I already assumed
That we're in the felony room
But I ain't a judge, you don't have to be nice to me
But please tell that
To your friend in the cowboy hat
You know he keeps on sayin' ev'rythin' twice to me
You know I was straight with you
You know I've never tried to change you in any way
You know if you didn't want to be with me
That you could...didn't have to stay

Now you stand here sayin' you forgive and forget. Honey, what can I say?
Yes, you, you just sit around and ask for ashtrays, can't you reach?
I see you kiss her on the cheek ev'rytime she gives a speech
With her picture books of the pyramid
And her postcards of Billy the Kid (why must everybody bow?)
You better talk to her 'bout it
You're her lover now

Oh, ev'rybody that cares
Is goin' up the castle stairs
But I'm not up in your castle, honey
It's true, I just can't recall
San Francisco at all
I can't even remember El Paso, uh, honey
You never had to be faithful
I didn't want you to grieve
Oh, why was it so hard for you
If you didn't want to be with me, just to leave?
Now you stand here while your finger's goin' up my sleeve
An' you, just what do you do anyway? Ain't there nothin' you can say?
She'll be standin' on the bar soon
With a fish head an' a harpoon
An' a fake beard plastered on her brow
You'd better do somethin' quick
She's your lover now

now all my fathers theyve gone down hugging one another
& all their daughters put me down cause i say i aint their brother

now all my fathers/ theyve gone down/ true love, they been without it
& all their sons & daughters put me down cause i dont think about it

here i stand
~~here i stand~~ i stand here
~~hoping~~ hoping that these frozen ships
that are ~~that are dance~~ dance madly up & down my lips
wont fall on you

约翰 · 韦斯利 · 哈丁
John Wesley Harding

胡续冬　译

1966 年 7 月 29 日，鲍勃 · 迪伦遭遇了一场摩托车祸，这在很大程度上改变了他的生活：一方面，死里逃生的经历以及两位民谣友人的相继骤然离世，让迪伦开始思考死亡；另一方面，他借此为由摆脱经纪人格罗斯曼（Albert Grossman）和出版商的压力，取消了六十四场美国巡演，并暂缓了《狼蛛》（*Tarantula*）的终审进程。在相对宽松的环境下，迪伦完成了个人第八张录音室专辑——《约翰 · 韦斯利 · 哈丁》。

这张发行于 1967 年 12 月 27 日、迪伦自称“与魔鬼交易”的专辑，乐器运用原声吉他，搭配口琴、钢琴，省却副歌的旋律，大部分歌词采取三段式的叙事形式，且不以时事作为主题。迪伦深入美国幽暗的秘史，重构那些早期冒险者的形象，在表现手法上突破伍迪 · 格思里对人物善恶分明的刻画，使之更为立体。

专辑同名歌曲，是迪伦为旧日美国西部法外之徒哈丁创作的一首叙事歌谣，颇有评论家将标题的首字母“JWH”解读为“耶和华”，但迪伦未曾承认歌名暗藏深意。不过，该专辑确实深受《圣经》影响，单从《我梦见我看到了圣奥古斯丁》《弗兰基·李和犹大祭司歌谣》《奸恶的使者》的歌名便能窥知，而《沿着瞭望塔》通篇歌词的意境，更是脱胎于《旧约·以赛亚书》。据迪伦母亲回忆，迪伦在这段车祸后的休养期间，他位于纽约州伍德斯托克镇新居中的最显眼处，总摊开着一本巨大的《圣经》，以便汲取灵感。

专辑浓厚的清教徒色彩，让嬉皮士深感错愕，却与美国的老历史相得益彰。另外，专辑中两首乡村色彩鲜明、温馨愉悦的作品——《沿着湾岸走》《今晚我将是你的宝贝》，则是下一张专辑风格的先声。

编者

约翰·韦斯利·哈丁[1]

约翰·韦斯利·哈丁
是穷人的朋友
他手持双枪闯荡
走遍了这片乡野
他打开过许多扇门
但从没听说他
欺负过老实人

在柴尼县那里
有次他们谈论说
他身边老是跟着他的情人
他出来表了个态
没多久那儿的局面
就都收拾好了
因为人所皆知他总是
乐于帮助别人

---

1. 约翰·韦斯利·哈丁（John Wesley Hardin，1853—1895），美国历史上的著名匪徒，迪伦故意将其姓 Hardin 误拼为 Harding。

在整份电报中
他的名字都无比响亮
但是对他的指控
没有一桩能被证实
这附近没有任何人
能够追踪他或是把他抓获
从未听说他
走错过半步

John Wesley Harding

John Wesley Harding
Was a friend to the poor
He trav'led with a gun in ev'ry hand
All along this countryside
He opened many a door
But he was never known
To hurt an honest man

'Twas down in Chaynee County
A time they talk about
With his lady by his side
He took a stand
And soon the situation there
Was all but straightened out
For he was always known
To lend a helping hand

All across the telegraph
His name it did resound
But no charge held against him
Could they prove
And there was no man around
Who could track or chain him down
He was never known
To make a foolish move

一天早晨，当我走出门

一天早晨，当我走出门
呼吸汤姆·潘恩[1]家附近的空气
我发现一个戴着镣铐行走的
最为美丽的姑娘
我把手递给她
她拉住了我的胳膊
那一瞬间我突然明白
她企图加害于我

“现在就从我身边走开”
我用我的声音对她说
她说：“可是我不愿意”
我说：“但是你没有选择”
“求求你了，先生”
她的嘴角发出请求
“我会偷偷接受你

---

1. 汤姆·潘恩，即托马斯·潘恩（Thomas Paine，1737—1809），英裔美国思想家、作家、政治活动家，曾参加美国独立运动和法国大革命。1963 年迪伦曾获托马斯·潘恩公民权利奖。

然后我们一起飞到南方去”

正在这时汤姆·潘恩本人
从田野对面跑了过来
冲着这个可爱的姑娘大喊
命令她退让
当她松开了手
汤姆·潘恩跑上前来，
“抱歉，先生，”他对我说
“我为她的所作所为感到抱歉”

As I Went Out One Morning

As I went out one morning
To breathe the air around Tom Paine's
I spied the fairest damsel
That ever did walk in chains
I offer'd her my hand
She took me by the arm
I knew that very instant
She meant to do me harm

"Depart from me this moment"
I told her with my voice
Said she, "But I don't wish to"
Said I, "But you have no choice"
"I beg you, sir," she pleaded
From the corners of her mouth
"I will secretly accept you
And together we'll fly south"

Just then Tom Paine, himself
Came running from across the field
Shouting at this lovely girl
And commanding her to yield
And as she was letting go her grip
Up Tom Paine did run
"I'm sorry, sir," he said to me
"I'm sorry for what she's done"

我梦见我看到了圣奥古斯丁

我梦见我看到了圣奥古斯丁
他像你我一样活着
在极度痛苦中
沿街流泪
有一条毯子在他胳膊之下
还有一件纯金的外套
正寻找着那些灵魂
已经全都被卖出了的

“起来吧，起来吧，”他大声喊着
声音毫无克制
“出来吧，无与伦比的君王和王后们
听听我悲伤的怨言
你们之中已经没有
属于你们自己的殉教者了
走你们自己该走的路吧
但是要知道你们并不孤独”

我梦见我看到了圣奥古斯丁
他活着，呼吸如火

我梦见我和其他人一起
把他逼上死路
哦，我带着怒气醒来
如此孤单，如此惊恐
我把手指紧贴在玻璃上
埋头哭泣

I Dreamed I Saw St. Augustine

I dreamed I saw St. Augustine
Alive as you or me
Tearing through these quarters
In the utmost misery
With a blanket underneath his arm
And a coat of solid gold
Searching for the very souls
Whom already have been sold

"Arise, arise," he cried so loud
In a voice without restraint
"Come out, ye gifted kings and queens
And hear my sad complaint
No martyr is among ye now
Whom you can call your own
So go on your way accordingly
But know you're not alone"

I dreamed I saw St. Augustine
Alive with fiery breath
And I dreamed I was amongst the ones
That put him out to death
Oh, I awoke in anger
So alone and terrified
I put my fingers against the glass
And bowed my head and cried

沿着瞭望塔

“一定有路离开这里，”小丑对小偷说
“这里困惑太多，我得不到解脱
生意人喝我的酒，庄稼汉挖我的土
他们当中没人知道其价值所在”

“没理由这么激动，”小偷友善地说
“这里有很多人觉得生活就是一个玩笑
但是你和我已经过了这个坎，这不是我们的命
所以我们别聊这些虚的了，时间不早了”

沿着瞭望塔，王子们一直在远望
女人们都来来去去，还有赤脚的仆人们

城外远处，一只野猫在咆哮
两名骑手渐近，风开始嚎叫

All Along the Watchtower

"There must be some way out of here," said the joker to the
thief
"There's too much confusion, I can't get no relief
Businessmen, they drink my wine, plowmen dig my earth
None of them along the line know what any of it is worth"

"No reason to get excited," the thief, he kindly spoke
"There are many here among us who feel that life is but
a joke
But you and I, we've been through that, and this is not our
fate
So let us not talk falsely now, the hour is getting late"

All along the watchtower, princes kept the view
While all the women came and went, barefoot servants, too

Outside in the distance a wildcat did growl
Two riders were approaching, the wind began to howl

弗兰基·李和犹大祭司歌谣

嗯，弗兰基·李和犹大祭司
他们是超级好的朋友
因此有一天弗兰基·李缺钱花了
犹大迅速掏出一卷十块钱
放在一把脚凳上
就在那片标绘的旷野里
他说："随便拿吧，弗兰基小兄弟
我的损失会变成你的收益"

嗯，弗兰基·李，他一屁股坐下
手指放在下巴上
但在犹大冰冷的目光下
他的脑袋开始犯晕
"请你别像这样盯着我看，"他说
"这只是我愚蠢的自尊心而已
但有些时候人必须独自去面对
躲也躲不掉"

嗯，犹大眨了眨眼，说
"好吧，我不打扰你了

但是你最好快点，在这些钞票消失前
选好你要拿哪些”
“我现在就开始拿了
告诉我你要去哪儿”
犹大指了指路
说：“去永恒！”

“永恒？”弗兰基·李说
声音像冰一样冷
“没错，”犹大祭司说，“永恒
你们可能管它叫‘天堂’”
“我不管它叫任何东西”
弗兰基·李笑着说
“好吧，”犹大祭司说
“我们一会儿见”

嗯，弗兰基·李又坐了回来
情绪低落，还有点局促
这时候走来一个陌生人
突然闯入画面中
他说：“你是弗兰基·李，
那个父亲已故的小赌徒吗？
如果你是的话，有个家伙在路上找你

他们说他是个祭司”

“哦，是的，他是我朋友”
受惊的弗兰基·李说
“我当然记得起他
事实上，他刚刚才离开我的视线”
“对，就是那个人，”陌生人说
他像老鼠一样平静
“好吧，我的口信是，他在这条路上
困在一栋房子里了”

嗯，弗兰基·李有点害怕
他丢下手里的东西就跑
一直跑到
犹大祭司所在的地方
“这是一栋什么房子啊，”他说
“我这是晃悠在什么地方？”
“这不是一栋房子，”犹大祭司说
“这不是一栋房子……这是一个家”

嗯，弗兰基·李颤抖了
很快他就对他内心中的一切
失去了控制

当教堂的钟声响起的时候
他只是呆立在那里盯着
那栋像任何恒星一样明亮的大房子
二十四扇窗户上
每扇都有一张女人的面孔

嗯，弗兰基·李
精神抖擞、连蹦带跳地跑上楼
他口吐白沫
开始让他的午夜悄然而动[1]
他胡言乱语了十六个日夜
但是在第十七天，他跌进了
犹大祭司的怀里
他就在那儿干渴而死

当人们笑嘻嘻地把他带走的时候
没人试图说点什么
当然，除了那个扛他去安息的
邻家小男孩
他孤零零地走着
把罪恶深深地隐藏起来

---

1. 让他的午夜悄然而动，意即“寻欢”。

呼吸中夹杂着咕哝

“啥都没暴露”

嗯，这个故事的寓意

这首歌的寓意

就是一个人绝不该去

不属于他的地方

因此当你看见你的邻居扛着东西的时候

请帮他一把

还有别把马路对面的家

错误地当成天堂

The Ballad of Frankie Lee and Judas Priest

Well, Frankie Lee and Judas Priest
They were the best of friends
So when Frankie Lee needed money one day
Judas quickly pulled out a roll of tens
And placed them on a footstool
Just above the plotted plain
Sayin', "Take your pick, Frankie Boy
My loss will be your gain"

Well, Frankie Lee, he sat right down
And put his fingers to his chin
But with the cold eyes of Judas on him
His head began to spin
"Would ya please not stare at me like that," he said
"It's just my foolish pride
But sometimes a man must be alone
And this is no place to hide"

Well, Judas, he just winked and said
"All right, I'll leave you here
But you'd better hurry up and choose which of those bills
you want
Before they all disappear"
"I'm gonna start my pickin' right now
Just tell me where you'll be"
Judas pointed down the road
And said, "Eternity!"

"Eternity?" said Frankie Lee

With a voice as cold as ice
"That's right," said Judas Priest, "Eternity
Though you might call it 'Paradise'"
"I don't call it anything"
Said Frankie Lee with a smile
"All right," said Judas Priest
"I'll see you after a while"

Well, Frankie Lee, he sat back down
Feelin' low and mean
When just then a passing stranger
Burst upon the scene
Saying, "Are you Frankie Lee, the gambler
Whose father is deceased?
Well, if you are, there's a fellow callin' you down the road
And they say his name is Priest"

"Oh, yes, he is my friend"
Said Frankie Lee in fright
"I do recall him very well
In fact, he just left my sight"
"Yes, that's the one," said the stranger
As quiet as a mouse
"Well, my message is, he's down the road
Stranded in a house"

Well, Frankie Lee, he panicked
He dropped ev'rything and ran
Until he came up to the spot
Where Judas Priest did stand
"What kind of house is this," he said
"Where I have come to roam?"
"It's not a house," said Judas Priest

"It's not a house...it's a home"

Well, Frankie Lee, he trembled
He soon lost all control
Over ev'rything which he had made
While the mission bells did toll
He just stood there staring
At that big house as bright as any sun
With four and twenty windows
And a woman's face in ev'ry one

Well, up the stairs ran Frankie Lee
With a soulful, bounding leap
And, foaming at the mouth
He began to make his midnight creep
For sixteen nights and days he raved
But on the seventeenth he burst
Into the arms of Judas Priest
Which is where he died of thirst

No one tried to say a thing
When they took him out in jest
Except, of course, the little neighbor boy
Who carried him to rest
And he just walked along, alone
With his guilt so well concealed
And muttered underneath his breath
"Nothing is revealed"

Well, the moral of the story
The moral of this song
Is simply that one should never be
Where one does not belong

So when you see your neighbor carryin' somethin'
Help him with his load
And don't go mistaking Paradise
For that home across the road

流浪汉的逃脱

“哦，救救我吧，我太脆弱”
我听见那个流浪汉这么说
他们架着他走出法庭
正要把他轰走
“我的旅行并不愉快
我时间不多了
我还不知道
我到底犯了什么错”

嗯，法官把法袍丢在一边
眼中含着一滴泪水
“你不能理解，”他说
“你为什么非要试着理解呢？”
外面的人群骚动了起来
你可以隔着门听见动静
里面，法官正走下来
而陪审团却在叫嚷该重判

“哦，让这该死的陪审团一边歇着去吧”
店员和看护喊道

“判决已经够糟糕了
但陪审团的表现还要糟糕十倍”
正在这时，一道闪电
把法庭劈垮
所有人跪下来祈祷的时候
流浪汉逃脱了

Drifter's Escape

"Oh, help me in my weakness"
I heard the drifter say
As they carried him from the courtroom
And were taking him away
"My trip hasn't been a pleasant one
And my time it isn't long
And I still do not know
What it was that I've done wrong"

Well, the judge, he cast his robe aside
A tear came to his eye
"You fail to understand," he said
"Why must you even try?"
Outside, the crowd was stirring
You could hear it from the door
Inside, the judge was stepping down
While the jury cried for more

"Oh, stop that cursed jury"
Cried the attendant and the nurse
"The trial was bad enough
But this is ten times worse"
Just then a bolt of lightning
Struck the courthouse out of shape
And while ev'rybody knelt to pray
The drifter did escape

亲爱的房东

亲爱的房东
请别为我的灵魂标价
我的负担太重
我的梦想已无法控制
当那艘蒸汽船的汽笛鸣响时
我会给你所有我该给的
我希望你能稳妥地收到
这取决于你如何去感受你的生活

亲爱的房东
请留意我说的这些话
我知道你受了很多苦
但是在这一点上你并不孤独
有时候，我们所有人或许都工作得过于努力
以至于不能过早、过多地拥有它
任何人都能够用他看得见的东西
填满生活，但他却不能触摸

亲爱的房东
别驳回我的意见

我不是来争论的

我也不准备搬到别处去

现在，我们中无论谁都有自己独特的天赋

你知道这肯定是对的

如果你不轻视我

我也不会轻视你

Dear Landlord

Dear landlord
Please don't put a price on my soul
My burden is heavy
My dreams are beyond control
When that steamboat whistle blows
I'm gonna give you all I got to give
And I do hope you receive it well
Dependin' on the way you feel that you live

Dear landlord
Please heed these words that I speak
I know you've suffered much
But in this you are not so unique
All of us, at times, we might work too hard
To have it too fast and too much
And anyone can fill his life up
With things he can see but he just cannot touch

Dear landlord
Please don't dismiss my case
I'm not about to argue
I'm not about to move to no other place
Now, each of us has his own special gift
And you know this was meant to be true
And if you don't underestimate me
I won't underestimate you

我是个寂寞的流浪汉

我是个寂寞的流浪汉
没有家庭，没有朋友
别人生活的起点
恰恰就是我生活的终点
我行过贿
敲过诈、骗过人
我服刑的罪名要啥有啥
除了沿街乞讨

嗯，我也曾经阔过
啥都不缺
嘴里镶着 14k 金
身上穿丝着绸
但是我不信任我的兄弟
总是对他斥责有加
这把我引向了可怕的厄运
在耻辱中浪迹四方

好心的女士们，先生们
我很快就走了

但是请让我在走之前
奉劝大家几句
切勿有丝毫的嫉妒心
不要按别人的套路过活
你要保留自己的判断
否则最终难免走上我这条路

I Am a Lonesome Hobo

I am a lonesome hobo
Without family or friends
Where another man's life might begin
That's exactly where mine ends
I have tried my hand at bribery
Blackmail and deceit
And I've served time for ev'rything
'Cept beggin' on the street

Well, once I was rather prosperous
There was nothing I did lack
I had fourteen-karat gold in my mouth
And silk upon my back
But I did not trust my brother
I carried him to blame
Which led me to my fatal doom
To wander off in shame

Kind ladies and kind gentlemen
Soon I will be gone
But let me just warn you all
Before I do pass on
Stay free from petty jealousies
Live by no man's code
And hold your judgment for yourself
Lest you wind up on this road

我同情这可怜的移民

我同情这可怜的移民
他宁愿还留在家乡
他用尽全力去作恶
但到头来往往还是孤身一人
这个人手指在作弊
每一道呼吸都在说谎
他恨死了他的生活
同时也惧怕死亡

我同情这可怜的移民
他白白浪费了精力
他的天堂有铁甲舰的形状
他挥泪如雨
他吃，但是吃不饱
他听，但是看不到
他爱上的是财富本身
对我不理不睬

我同情这可怜的移民
他踏了一路的泥浆

他的嘴里塞满了笑声
他用鲜血建造他的城市
这城市最终的景象
一定会像玻璃一样粉碎
我同情这可怜的移民
当他的欢乐得以兑现

I Pity the Poor Immigrant

I pity the poor immigrant
Who wishes he would've stayed home
Who uses all his power to do evil
But in the end is always left so alone
That man whom with his fingers cheats
And who lies with ev'ry breath
Who passionately hates his life
And likewise, fears his death

I pity the poor immigrant
Whose strength is spent in vain
Whose heaven is like Ironsides
Whose tears are like rain
Who eats but is not satisfied
Who hears but does not see
Who falls in love with wealth itself
And turns his back on me

I pity the poor immigrant
Who tramples through the mud
Who fills his mouth with laughing
And who builds his town with blood
Whose visions in the final end
Must shatter like the glass
I pity the poor immigrant
When his gladness comes to pass

奸恶的使者[1]

有一个奸恶的使者
从以利[2]那处来
他善于把最小的事情夸大
当被问到谁找他来时
他用拇指来回答
因为他的舌头不会说话，只会奉承

他待在大厅后面
在那儿他搭了个床铺
经常可以看见他回来
直到有一天，他出现时
手里拿着一张纸，写着
“我发誓，我的脚底在燃烧”

哦，树叶开始飘落
海洋开始分开

1.《旧约 · 箴言》13:17：“奸恶的使者必陷在祸患里；忠信的使臣乃医人的良药。”此注译文引自和合本。

2. 以利，《旧约 · 撒母耳记》里的士师与大祭司。当报信人告知以色列人被非利士人打败，以利二子皆死，耶和华的约柜被掳，以利从座位上往后跌倒而死。

他面前有人群涌动

他只被告知了这一句

戳中他心底的话

“如果你不能带来好消息，就啥也别带了”

The Wicked Messenger

There was a wicked messenger
From Eli he did come
With a mind that multiplied the smallest matter
When questioned who had sent for him
He answered with his thumb
For his tongue it could not speak, but only flatter

He stayed behind the assembly hall
It was there he made his bed
Oftentimes he could be seen returning
Until one day he just appeared
With a note in his hand which read
"The soles of my feet, I swear they're burning"

Oh, the leaves began to fallin'
And the seas began to part
And the people that confronted him were many
And he was told but these few words
Which opened up his heart
"If ye cannot bring good news, then don't bring any"

沿着湾岸走

沿着湾岸走
我瞅见我的真爱朝我走来
沿着湾岸走
我瞅见我的真爱朝我走来
我说："天可怜见，妹子
今儿看见你走过来真是太好了"

沿着湾岸走
我瞅见我的极乐小妞
沿着湾岸走
我瞅见我的极乐小妞
她说："天可怜见，甜心
你做我的男朋友我真开心！"

沿着湾岸走
我们手拉手一起漫步
沿着湾岸走
我们手拉手一起漫步
每个人都看着我们走过
他们知道我们好上了，嗯，他们都懂

Down Along the Cove

Down along the cove
I spied my true love comin' my way
Down along the cove
I spied my true love comin' my way
I say, "Lord, have mercy, mama
It sure is good to see you comin' today"

Down along the cove
I spied my little bundle of joy
Down along the cove
I spied my little bundle of joy
She said, "Lord, have mercy, honey
I'm so glad you're my boy!"

Down along the cove
We walked together hand in hand
Down along the cove
We walked together hand in hand
Ev'rybody watchin' us go by
Knows we're in love, yes, and they understand

沿着湾岸走
（另一版本）

沿着湾岸走我瞅见我的极乐小妞
沿着湾岸走我瞅见我的极乐小妞
我说："天可怜见，宝贝儿
你让我感觉自己像个小毛孩儿"

沿着湾岸走一大群人在瞎转悠
沿着湾岸走一大群人在瞎转悠
我说："天可怜见，宝贝儿，你往上他们会撞你
你往下，他们会踢你"

沿着湾岸走我感觉像鸟儿在高飞
沿着湾岸走我感觉像鸟儿在高飞
我说："天可怜见，宝贝儿
为什么你每次都只说一个词儿？"

沿着湾岸走我看见了水手们和河流女王号[1]

---

1. 河流女王号，19 世纪末的蒸汽渡轮。美国内战期间曾作为当时陆军上将尤利西斯·格兰特（Ulysses S. Grant）的专用通信船。1911 年退役。

沿着湾岸走我看见了水手们和河流女王号
我说："天可怜见，宝贝儿
那算不算你见过的最大的船？"

沿着湾岸走，你可以放下你所有的钱
沿着湾岸走，你可以放下你所有的钱
我说："天可怜见，宝贝儿
他们把你推来推去任意摆布是不是太无耻？"

沿着湾岸走，我提着我的行李箱
沿着湾岸走，我提着我的行李箱
我说："天可怜见，宝贝儿
我是你的男人，你会不会很开心？"

Down Along the Cove
(Alternate Version)

Down along the cove I spied my little bundle of joy
Down along the cove I spied my little bundle of joy
I said, "Lord have mercy, baby
You make me feel just like a baby boy"

Down along the cove a bunch of people are milling around
Down along the cove a bunch of people are milling around
I said, "Lord have mercy, baby, they're gonna knock you when you're up
They're gonna kick you when you're down"

Down along the cove I feel as high as a bird
Down along the cove I feel as high as a bird
I said, "Lord have mercy, baby
How come you never say more than a word?"

Down along the cove I seen the Jacks and the River Queen
Down along the cove I seen the Jacks and the River Queen
I said, "Lord have mercy, baby
Ain't that the biggest boat you ever seen?"

Down along the cove, you can lay all your money down
Down along the cove, you can lay all your money down
I said, "Lord have mercy, baby
Ain't it a shame how they shove you and they push you around?"

Down along the cove, I got my suitcase in my hand
Down along the cove, I got my suitcase in my hand
I said, "Lord have mercy, baby
Ain't you glad that I'm your man?"

今晚我将是你的宝贝

闭上你的眼睛，关上门
你再也不用担心什么
今晚我将是你的宝贝

关上灯，拉上帘子
你再也不用害怕
今晚我将是你的宝贝

嗯，那只反舌鸟要飞走了
我们会忘记它
那只巨大、肥胖的月亮会像勺子一样闪亮
但我们会由它去
你不会后悔

踢掉你的鞋子，别怕
把酒放在这儿
今晚我将是你的宝贝

I'll Be Your Baby Tonight

Close your eyes, close the door
You don't have to worry anymore
I'll be your baby tonight

Shut the light, shut the shade
You don't have to be afraid
I'll be your baby tonight

Well, that mockingbird's gonna sail away
We're gonna forget it
That big, fat moon is gonna shine like a spoon
But we're gonna let it
You won't regret it

Kick your shoes off, do not fear
Bring that bottle over here
I'll be your baby tonight

1. Throw my ticket out the window
Throw my suitcase out there too
Throw my troubles out the door -
I don't need them anymore
Cause tonight I'm staying here with you

纳什维尔天际线
Nashville Skyline

奚密　译

《纳什维尔天际线》是鲍勃 · 迪伦的第九张专辑，1969 年 4 月 9 日由哥伦比亚唱片公司发行。纳什维尔是美国乡村音乐的发源地，专辑名字便表明了迪伦这批歌曲的风格取向——它们的灵感不是来自民谣或摇滚，而是乡村音乐。当时迪伦的摇滚作品风靡欧美，其乐坛地位无人可以取替，因此,《纳什维尔天际线》的转向颇为耐人寻味。专辑的封面照是笑得开怀的迪伦;里面的情歌一反迪伦过去的嘲讽与苦涩，充满了温馨与包容;而他温柔抒情的歌声也不同于前面的几张专辑。

但迪伦就是迪伦,《纳什维尔天际线》并非一般意义上的乡村音乐。它的原创性在于把摇滚和乡村音乐相结合，打破了当时的成见。其歌词虽简单直接，但在接受美国《新闻周刊》杂志的采访时，迪伦坦承，比起此前的作品，这批乡村歌曲流露了更多的自我。此专辑共收录了迪伦的十首作品，除与著名乡村歌手约翰尼·卡什(Johnny Cash)合唱的《北国女孩》(*Girl from the North Country*）之外，其余九首均收入全集之中。其中《与你单独一起》《我将它全抛弃》《躺下，淑女，躺下》更成为乡村摇滚的经典。

20 世纪 60 年代后期，美国正值多事之秋，先是 1968 年 4 月 4 日民权运动领袖马丁 · 路德 · 金遭到暗杀；两个月后，参议员、前总统之弟罗伯特 · 肯尼迪（Robert F. Kennedy）亦被行刺身亡。然而《纳什维尔天际线》却不触及任何社会政治议题，这与迪伦早期的作品形成强烈对比。此中可能有两个原因。第一，1966 年 7 月 29 日迪伦在回家的路上发生了摩托车意外。在此后长达八年的时间里，他极少进行巡回演出，也因此得以享受宁静的私人生活。第二，20 世纪 60 年代中期的迪伦被推为美国叛逆一代和社会抗议歌手的代表，他对此深感不耐，更是厌烦这种定型。多年后他回忆起这段岁月时说，年轻的他既不想要，更不需要强加于他身上的标签。《纳什维尔天际线》可以说是迪伦一份回归自我、清新快乐的佐证。

奚密

与你单独在一起

与你单独在一起
只有你和我
你就不能给我一句真话吗?
难道不该这样吗?
我俩紧紧地相拥
整晚整夜都如此
一切永远是对的
当我与你单独在一起

与你单独在一起
当白日即将结束
眼中只有一个你
当黄昏渐渐溜走
这仅仅表明了
人生的喜悦不多
我唯一知道的
就是与你单独在一起

他们说黑夜才是好时光
和心爱的人一起度过

白天有太多干扰的念头
但是你让我不断思念
我渴望着黑夜来临
带来你的千娇百媚
只有你在我的身旁
将我拥入你的怀抱

我会永远感谢上帝
当白日的工作结束
我得到的甜蜜报酬
是与你单独在一起

To Be Alone with You

To be alone with you
Just you and me
Now won't you tell me true
Ain't that the way it oughta be?
To hold each other tight
The whole night through
Ev'rything is always right
When I'm alone with you

To be alone with you
At the close of the day
With only you in view
While evening slips away
It only goes to show
That while life's pleasures be few
The only one I know
Is when I'm alone with you

They say that nighttime is the right time
To be with the one you love
Too many thoughts get in the way in the day
But you're always what I'm thinkin' of
I wish the night were here
Bringin' me all of your charms
When only you are near
To hold me in your arms

I'll always thank the Lord
When my working day's through

I get my sweet reward
To be alone with you

我将它全抛弃

我曾经将她拥在怀里
她说她永远不会离去
但是我太残酷
把她当傻瓜般对待
我将它全抛弃

我曾经掌中握着山岳
和日复一日流过的河流
我一定是疯了
一直不明白我拥有的
直到我将它全抛弃

爱是一切，爱让地球运转
爱而且只有爱，不能被否定
不管你对它有什么想法
没有它你真的束手无策
劝你接受过来人的提示

所以如果你找到一个全心全意爱你的人
要珍惜于心，别让爱离你而去

因为有一件事可以肯定

你将会伤得很深

如果你将它全抛弃

I Threw It All Away

I once held her in my arms
She said she would always stay
But I was cruel
I treated her like a fool
I threw it all away

Once I had mountains in the palm of my hand
And rivers that ran through ev'ry day
I must have been mad
I never knew what I had
Until I threw it all away

Love is all there is, it makes the world go 'round
Love and only love, it can't be denied
No matter what you think about it
You just won't be able to do without it
Take a tip from one who's tried

So if you find someone that gives you all of her love
Take it to your heart, don't let it stray
For one thing that's certain
You will surely be a-hurtin'
If you throw it all away

佩姬·白日[1]

佩姬·白日偷走了我可怜的心
老天啊，我又能说什么
想和佩姬·白日共度黑夜

夜里的佩姬让我的未来多光明
兄弟，这女郎好得简直举世无双
想和夜里的佩姬共度白日

嗯，你知道甚至在我连她的名字都没听过以前
你知道我就一样地爱着她了
我告诉所有的人不管我走到哪儿
他们要知道她是我的小女人
我是如此地爱着她

佩姬·白日偷走了我可怜的心
把我的天空从灰色变成蓝色
想和佩姬·白日共度黑夜

---

1. 佩姬·白日，音译作“佩姬·戴”，为保留原作中日与夜的呼应，故作此译。

佩姬·白日偷走了我可怜的心
老天啊，我还能说什么呢
想和佩姬·白日共度黑夜
想和佩姬·白日共度黑夜

Peggy Day

Peggy Day stole my poor heart away
By golly, what more can I say
Love to spend the night with Peggy Day

Peggy night makes my future look so bright
Man, that girl is out of sight
Love to spend the day with Peggy night

Well, you know that even before I learned her name
You know I loved her just the same
An' I tell 'em all, wherever I may go
Just so they'll know, that she's my little lady
And I love her so

Peggy Day stole my poor heart away
Turned my skies to blue from gray
Love to spend the night with Peggy Day

Peggy Day stole my poor heart away
By golly, what more can I say
Love to spend the night with Peggy Day
Love to spend the night with Peggy Day

躺下，淑女，躺下

躺下，淑女，躺下，躺在我大大的铜床上
躺下，淑女，躺下，躺在我大大的铜床上
不管哪些色彩浮现在你的脑海中
我会展示它们让你看见它们闪耀

躺下，淑女，躺下，躺在我大大的铜床上
留下，淑女，留下，陪你的男人一会儿吧
直到天亮，让我看见你带给他笑容
他的衣服肮脏但是他的双手洁净
而你是他见过的事物中最美好的

留下，淑女，留下，陪你的男人一会儿吧
为何继续等待着这个世界的开始
鱼与熊掌两者兼得又有何不可呢
为何继续等待着你的真爱的出现
此时此刻他不就站在你的面前吗

躺下，淑女，躺下，躺在我大大的铜床上
留下，淑女，留下，留下因为夜还长着呢
我渴望在晨光中看见你

我渴望在夜里触摸到你

留下，淑女，留下，留下因为夜还长着呢

Lay, Lady, Lay

Lay, lady, lay, lay across my big brass bed
Lay, lady, lay, lay across my big brass bed
Whatever colors you have in your mind
I'll show them to you and you'll see them shine

Lay, lady, lay, lay across my big brass bed
Stay, lady, stay, stay with your man awhile
Until the break of day, let me see you make him smile
His clothes are dirty but his hands are clean
And you're the best thing that he's ever seen

Stay, lady, stay, stay with your man awhile
Why wait any longer for the world to begin
You can have your cake and eat it too
Why wait any longer for the one you love
When he's standing in front of you

Lay, lady, lay, lay across my big brass bed
Stay, lady, stay, stay while the night is still ahead
I long to see you in the morning light
I long to reach for you in the night
Stay, lady, stay, stay while the night is still ahead

又是一个夜晚

又是一个夜晚，众星入眼
但是今夜的我比谁都寂寞
哦，月光那么皎洁
照亮了眼中的一切
但是今夜没有光为我照亮

哦，遗憾悲哀我失去了唯一的好友
我就是无法成为她心目中的那个我
我会把头仰得高高的
面向滚滚的黑暗天色
因为今夜没有光为我照亮

当初以为她会忠贞是个天大的错误
我不懂恋爱中的女人会干些什么事！

又是一个夜晚，我等待月光
当一阵微风高高拂过树梢
哦，我多么思念我的爱人
我不是有意让她那样离去的
但是今夜没有光为我照亮

又是一个夜晚，月光那么皎洁
而一阵微风高高拂过树梢
哦，我多么思念我的爱人
我不是有意让她那样离去的
但是今夜没有光为我照亮

One More Night

One more night, the stars are in sight
But tonight I'm as lonesome as can be
Oh, the moon is shinin' bright
Lighting ev'rything in sight
But tonight no light will shine on me

Oh, it's shameful and it's sad I lost the only pal I had
I just could not be what she wanted me to be
I will turn my head up high
To that dark and rolling sky
For tonight no light will shine on me

I was so mistaken when I thought that she'd be true
I had no idea what a woman in love would do!

One more night, I will wait for the light
While the wind blows high above the tree
Oh, I miss my darling so
I didn't mean to see her go
But tonight no light will shine on me

One more night, the moon is shinin' bright
And the wind blows high above the tree
Oh, I miss that woman so
I didn't mean to see her go
But tonight no light will shine on me

告诉我那不是真的

镇上的谣言满天飞
他们说你要抛弃我
我只请你做一件事
告诉我那不是真的

他们说看见你跟别的男人在一起
他又高又帅褐色的肌肤，你牵着他的手
亲爱的，我指望你
告诉我那不是真的

想到别的男人正紧紧拥抱着你
我就全身疼痛，这太没道理

我听到所有那些糟糕的事
我都不想信，我只想听你说
所以亲爱的，你最好办得到
告诉我那不是真的

我听到所有那些糟糕的事
我都不想信，我只想听你说

所以亲爱的，我指望你

告诉我那不是真的

Tell Me That It Isn't True

I have heard rumors all over town
They say that you're planning to put me down
All I would like you to do
Is tell me that it isn't true

They say that you've been seen with some other man
That he's tall, dark and handsome, and you're holding his hand
Darlin', I'm a-countin' on you
Tell me that it isn't true

To know that some other man is holdin' you tight
It hurts me all over, it doesn't seem right

All of those awful things that I have heard
I don't want to believe them, all I want is your word
So darlin', you better come through
Tell me that it isn't true

All of those awful things that I have heard
I don't want to believe them, all I want is your word
So darlin', I'm countin' on you
Tell me that it isn't true

乡村水果派

就像吹萨克斯风的老乔
当他灌下了一桶酒
天啊，我的妈呀
我爱乡村水果派

听那个小提琴手拉着琴
一拉就拉到大天亮
天啊，我的妈呀
我爱乡村水果派

红莓草莓黄柠檬绿柠檬
我又在乎啥?
蓝莓苹果樱桃南瓜李子
叫我吃晚餐，蜜糖，我就来

给我的大白鹅备好鞍
把我绑上后任它奔跑
天啊，我的妈呀
我爱乡村水果派

说实话我需要的并不多
我又不是在赛跑
给我一个乡村水果派
我不会吐在别人脸上

那棵老桃树给我摇一摇
小杰克·霍纳[1]也奈何不了我
天啊，我的妈呀
我爱乡村水果派

1. 指涉英语童谣《小杰克·霍纳》："小杰克·霍纳 / 坐在墙旮旯，/ 吃着圣诞派。"

Country Pie

Just like old Saxophone Joe
When he's got the hogshead up on his toe
Oh me, oh my
Love that country pie

Listen to the fiddler play
When he's playin' 'til the break of day
Oh me, oh my
Love that country pie

Raspberry, strawberry, lemon and lime
What do I care?
Blueberry, apple, cherry, pumpkin and plum
Call me for dinner, honey, I'll be there

Saddle me up my big white goose
Tie me on 'er and turn her loose
Oh me, oh my
Love that country pie

I don't need much and that ain't no lie
Ain't runnin' any race
Give to me my country pie
I won't throw it up in anybody's face

Shake me up that old peach tree
Little Jack Horner's got nothin' on me
Oh me, oh my
Love that country pie

今夜我在这儿陪伴你

把我的车票扔出窗外
把我的行李也全扔掉
把我的烦恼抛到门外
这些东西我不再需要
因为今夜我会在这儿陪伴你

本来今早我该离开小镇
但我就是做不到
哦，你的爱来得这么强烈
让我整天痴痴等待
等待今夜我会在这儿陪伴你

这有什么好奇怪的呢
陌生人可能得到的一份爱
你施魔法让我臣服其下
我发现离开竟是如此困难

我可以听到汽笛鸣叫
我也看见车站站长
如果街上有个穷小伙子

就把我的座位让给他
因为今夜我会在这儿陪伴你

把我的车票扔出窗外
把我的行李也全扔掉
把我的烦恼抛到门外
这些东西我不再需要
因为今夜我会在这儿陪伴你

Tonight I'll Be Staying Here with You

Throw my ticket out the window
Throw my suitcase out there, too
Throw my troubles out the door
I don't need them anymore
'Cause tonight I'll be staying here with you

I should have left this town this morning
But it was more than I could do
Oh, your love comes on so strong
And I've waited all day long
For tonight when I'll be staying here with you

Is it really any wonder
The love that a stranger might receive
You cast your spell and I went under
I find it so difficult to leave

I can hear that whistle blowin'
I see that stationmaster, too
If there's a poor boy on the street
Then let him have my seat
'Cause tonight I'll be staying here with you

Throw my ticket out the window
Throw my suitcase out there, too
Throw my troubles out the door
I don't need them anymore
'Cause tonight I'll be staying here with you

通缉犯

加利福尼亚州的通缉犯，水牛城的通缉犯
堪萨斯城的通缉犯，俄亥俄州的通缉犯
密西西比州的通缉犯，老夏延市的通缉犯
今晚不管你朝哪儿看，你都有可能看到这个通缉犯

也许我在科罗拉多州或滨海的佐治亚州
我打工的老板或许对我的身世一无所知
如果你看见我走过来而且认出我是谁
别透露给别人因为你知道我是个在逃犯

露西·沃森追缉的人，珍妮·布朗追缉的人
内莉·约翰逊追缉的人，下一个小镇追缉的人
但是我已经拥有我所要的许多许多东西
远远多于我所需要的、后来坏掉的那些东西

在埃尔帕索我走上岔路，停车找份地图
误入华雷斯怀里抱着胡安妮塔
然后在什里夫波特睡着，在阿比林醒来
奇怪在某两个城镇之间我怎么就变成了个通缉犯

阿尔伯克基的通缉犯，锡拉丘兹的通缉犯
塔拉哈西的通缉犯，巴吞鲁日的通缉犯
不管我走到哪里，总有人想动手抓我
今晚不管你朝哪里看，你都有可能瞅到我呢

加利福尼亚州的通缉犯，水牛城的通缉犯
堪萨斯城的通缉犯，俄亥俄州的通缉犯
密西西比州的通缉犯，老夏延市的通缉犯
今晚不管你朝哪儿看，你都有可能看到这个通缉犯

Wanted Man

Wanted man in California, wanted man in Buffalo
Wanted man in Kansas City, wanted man in Ohio
Wanted man in Mississippi, wanted man in old Cheyenne
Wherever you might look tonight, you might see this wanted man

I might be in Colorado or Georgia by the sea
Working for some man who may not know at all who I might be
If you ever see me comin' and if you know who I am
Don't you breathe it to nobody 'cause you know I'm on the lam

Wanted man by Lucy Watson, wanted man by Jeannie Brown
Wanted man by Nellie Johnson, wanted man in this next town
But I've had all that I've wanted of a lot of things I had
And a lot more than I needed of some things that turned out bad

I got sidetracked in El Paso, stopped to get myself a map
Went the wrong way into Juarez with Juanita on my lap
Then I went to sleep in Shreveport, woke up in Abilene
Wonderin' why the hell I'm wanted at some town halfway between

Wanted man in Albuquerque, wanted man in Syracuse
Wanted man in Tallahassee, wanted man in Baton Rouge

There's somebody set to grab me anywhere that I might be
And wherever you might look tonight, you might get a
glimpse of me

Wanted man in California, wanted man in Buffalo
Wanted man in Kansas City, wanted man in Ohio
Wanted man in Mississippi, wanted man in old Cheyenne
Wherever you might look tonight, you might see this
wanted man